NOTTI PINE AND THE DREAMTIME

By
Cherie Andrea Hamilton

There once lived an honorable and elderly man of meager means, with only one wish. He wished for all who lived in the present, near and far, to learn the art of communicating with their ancestors through the magical portal known as the dreamtime. For in doing so, one would receive guidance and knowledge from an ancient and wise source.

TABLE OF CONTENTS

Prologue

"Open for me now, for I am War Ma the tomb keeper and master of this lock," ordered the king of Atlas. He stood proudly robbed in royal blue with one arm holding a lit torch, and the other holding a large purple crystal above his polished bald head. Slowly, he waved the crystal before the great doors and recited his chant.

"Gem of motion and gem of release, open this domain and allow me to enter."

His words echoed through the halls and burst out of the chamber entrance into the arid river valley. Waiting in the shadows stood two elders with dimpled cheeks and crooked smiles. Together they held a large, sealed gold disk, which caused each to tremble slightly from the weight. A trickle of sweat dripped down the forehead of one, while the other held his breath in anticipation.

A loud clank from the opening of the double doors sent a tremble of fear through them. They watched as a gust of ancient dust turned into a dark cloud. It then blew by them with a loud whistle. War Ma raised the flaming torch and stepped inside the tomb.

He searched until a stone slab caught his eye. Behind the slab appeared a wall of shelves filled with ornaments, bowls, and sculptures. With respect he looked at the stone carved birds, such as Hawk the messenger and Raven the carrier of magic.

A booming voice echoed from the darkness and War Ma took a step back.

"Have you come to free me from my eternal prison?" bellowed a commanding voice.

"Yes," said War Ma. "I have come to offer you my assistance to reclaim your throne."

War Ma raised the torch and gasped at the sight of Lord Seb, wrapped completely in a white cloth and floating high above the flat stone. A giant serpent of protection moved into position, only inches from War Ma's face and shot out its tongue at him.

"What is your plan?" questioned Lord Seb. He shot out a red beam of light from his fingertip toward the serpent, who quickly lowered its head to the ground. Shaken, War Ma took another step back and motioned to his attendants.

"Ban and Jab, please enter!"

With their heads bowed, the two men entered the eerie domain carrying a large clay seat. Ban huffed with each step, and his dimpled cheeks emptied and filled with each breath like a trumpet player. Jab's cheeks remained filled as he continued to hold his breath. Carefully they set down the chair and stood at attention.

"Lord Seb, we have Lady Oshun who governs and protects the land of the fertile river valley. We have brought her here for you to use as ransom for our demands," said War Ma as he puffed up his chest like a proud rooster ready to announce the morning sun.

Lord Seb floated over them and responded with such boldness that War Ma teetered backwards and almost fell.

"To kidnap a member of the sacred temple of the ancestors is an offense. Why go against temple law?"

War Ma regained his composure and took one confident step forward before stating his plea.

"I, and the dedicated elders who wait to serve you, knew of no other way. We have worked patiently for this moment to not only capture Lady Oshun who offers guidance for the fertility of the farmland, but to find you by obtaining the gemstone key from your saboteurs."

"Continue," whispered Lord Seb with an intriguing eye.

"With the death of King Mano, we will declare to the young heir and to his governing mother, that drought will come if your name is not reinstated as lord of the blessed dead. Furthermore, we will decree that all references and images of you as an enemy, a murderer, and evil, be abolished and erased from the ancestral texts, for they are lies. Finally, we will declare that all dreamtime bracelets be relinquished until the true history of your authority can be restored."

Lord Seb nodded several times, and although his face remained covered, War Ma knew he was somberly remembering the pain and the humiliation of being cast from the temple and replaced by the authority of the mortal king.

"Put Lady Oshun on the platform," ordered the lord.

War Ma motioned for the attendants to move her. Trembling, they took careful steps around the serpent before setting the vessel down. With bowed heads, they shuffled out to wait.

Lord Seb floated over Lady Oshun while listening to her faint lamenting. He shook his head with apparent concern.

"No harm will come to you my lady, for one day I will earn your forgiveness."

War Ma removed his blue hooded cloak and held it up for his lord. Majestically, Lord Seb floated down and allowed his shoulders to be draped and covered.

"We have a boat waiting to take you to our most talented physicians who are ready to restore your being," said War Ma with a hint of enthusiasm.

"Yes of course," replied Lord Seb. "Your attendants will guard the doors until daily replacements can be assigned, and my trusted serpent will stay on guard until my return," he concluded with renewed authority and relief.

With confinement, he had become lonely and desperate over the many long years. He could only imagine how his disappearance had impacted on the beings of the world. Especially for those who would have received his guidance from life until death. For without this process, how would one know the next mission, purpose, or even the lessons learned to become a being of light?

He consoled himself, knowing he would one day find a way to restore the sacredness of this human passage. Pulling the cloak tighter around his chest, he fought back his sadness. He rocked himself back and forth like a child in his own mother's arms.

"It will be fine; it will all be fine. Now that I am free, I will find a way," he whispered to his aching heart.

They departed the tomb, and the great doors boomed shut and the lit torches flickered. The attendants were left to stand in their own shadows to guard Lady Oshun.

Grandpa Pine closed his eyes and whispered.

"Receive and remember what I have seen my love; for the sake of our dear granddaughter."

He opened his eyes and heard the gentle rippling of water from the oars, signaling the sailing ship's departure.

Chapter One

GRANDPA PINE'S VISIT

The grandfather clock struck the hour of four, followed by four continuous echoing chimes. Grandma Pine awoke, sat up, and rubbed the dream from her eyes. "Lord Seb?" she whispered. She climbed out of bed and put on her plush pink bathrobe before stepping into each moccasin.

Down the stairs she looped into the kitchen. She pondered over the dream and wondered why she had dreamed of Lord Seb. Opening the refrigerator door, the light struck her perplexed face. She grabbed the bottle of beet juice from the top shelf.

"He wants Notti to know," she said.

She poured the juice into her favorite floral mug. George's words echoed in her thoughts as she took a long sip. "Ah, that tastes good," she said thinking of his loving smile.

"Why did you leave me? It's only been a few months, but I miss you so much." The tears spilled over her cheeks. Wiping them away with the sash of her robe, she imagined George drinking his morning coffee. He always drank the ground dark roasted bean coffee with a dash of cream and a teaspoon of sugar. Just like a milk shake he would say after the first sip. And of course, he would have a bite of his jelly donut or cinnamon roll next.

"Oh, I wish you were here," she whispered, patting her hand over her heart.

"I need you, George."

The air stood almost silent and still. The ticking of the clock reminded her of what her mother had told her as a child. That right before dawn is a time where your mind, heart, and spirit can invite anything into being. She was never sure what her mother meant. So, she decided it was a time when wishes and dreams could come true. A ray of moonlight struck the juice bottle and suddenly the light began to expand. Grandma Pine watched in awe as the beam of light grew to fill the kitchen. She almost dropped her mug when from the light a ghostly George emerged. He smiled with his dimpled cheek and happy eyes.

Grandma Pine leaned back but cautiously reached for him with her finger. She watched it go right through his shoulder. Disappointed, she quickly withdrew her hand.

"George, is it really you?"

The light surrounding him buzzed like a fluorescent bulb, and he nodded.

"Where have you been? I've been worried about you, wondering if you made it to the ancestral realm or not."

Grandpa Pine gave his widow a reassuring smile.

"George, I had a dream about Lord Seb. Did you send me that dream?" George nodded with a grave look.

"Is this about Notti?" He nodded again, but this time he smiled.

"Remember when you first told me about the dreamtime" she asked with a look of concern? His smile widened.

"And when Notti was born you knew she would be the one to learn the ancient ways, didn't you?"

George nodded again before taking a sip of his ghostly coffee.

"How unfortunate it's been to have kept the dreamtime a secret from her. Even with all our son's academic knowledge, he still won't believe in the possibility."

George lowered his head. He took a moment to acknowledge the loss of passing the ancient practice to their only son.

"What do you want to do? I know you want me to help Notti," asked Grandma Pine.

George opened his hand, and on his palm appeared a silver bracelet with a garnet gem.

"Of course, but do you want me to give it to her?"

He nodded and placed the bracelet in her extended open hand.

"Remember to tell Notti how to use it," said Grandpa Pine.

And with a wink he blew her a kiss, and in an instant disappeared.

"George, come back, don't leave me," she whispered, patting her other hand over her heart.

She felt gratitude for her moment with her best friend, and beloved eternal partner. She also felt confident that she would find a way to introduce Notti to the dreamtime. She would help Notti understand. as she put the bracelet into her bathrobe pocket.

Finishing her juice, she rose and stretched the tightness from her shoulders. Glancing at the clock, she noticed how no time had passed with Grandpa's visit. Odd, she thought as she gazed through the picture window at the full moon. By the end of the week its fullness would blanket their home with its illuminating beauty.

Back up the stairs she crept to her room, thinking of George with every step. Wishing he hadn't been so stubborn about seeing a doctor when his condition worsened. She placed the bracelet in her jewelry box. Then hung up her robe and slipped under the covers. Soon she fell asleep. And began snoring as loud as a tuba player in a marching band.

Chapter Two

A TIME TO GO

The sun rose, sending delicate rays on Grandma Pine's face. She slept soundly in the quiet city of New Haven. The doorbell suddenly chimed with the clock reading 9:35 a.m. She got up remembering George's visit and quickly put on her robe. She took out the bracelet from the jewelry box and put it in her pocket. The bell rang again, and she hurried down the stairs to the front door.

Unlocking the half dozen locks and bolts, she turned off the alarm and pulled on the door knob. There stood Notti, beaming with a welcoming smile and a dimple just like her grandpa's.

"Good morning, Grandma, we're packed and ready to leave for Dad's new job," said Notti. She pointed to their green and white van parked on the busy curb. Grandma Pine looked at her son Terence sitting behind the steering wheel puffing on his pipe. And her daughter-in-law Annette sat beside him inspecting a large map. In the back seats were toddlers Rusty and Randy. They were eating dry cereal from a cup and watching \all the people passing by. On top of the van, hung green plastic tarps covering a large pile of luggage and Terence's guitar.

"Hello Mother "greeted Terence as he stepped out of the van.

"We thought we'd get an early start. It's a two-day drive, and Notti has already missed a week of school,"

Grandma Pine held back her tears and hugged her only granddaughter.

"You be a good girl and send me letters. Come back to visit me when school's out."

"Okay, I will," said Notti as her eyes rested on the whale bone pendant hung around Grandma's neck. Grandpa bought the necklace from a petite Māori woman from New Zealand at an international market in New York City. The woman told Grandpa that the figure eight represents eternity. When Grandpa put the necklace on Grandma, he told her that he would love her for all eternity. Notti wondered if he could still love her even though he was now gone.

"Notti," said Grandma Pine, glancing at her son who was shaking hands with Mr. Champ, the president of the historical society.

"Notti, listen," she said looking into her granddaughter's brown cheerful eyes.   She held her hand and placed the bracelet around Notti's wrist.

"This is a dreamtime bracelet gift from Grandpa. When you're ready to go to sleep, think of your grandpa."

"Okay, Grandma I will remember him reading me a story."

"Good, and with this bracelet you will travel somewhere in a dream while thinking of Grandpa. Will you remember to do that Sweetheart?"

Grandma Pine glanced at her son again taking to neighbor Mr. Champ who wished him the best of luck.

"Okay Grandma, I will," answered Notti with a curious shrug.

"Good, because it's very important. Promise me that if you have a dream of Grandpa and a dreamtime place, that you'll remember it and tell me when I phone you," she said.

Grandma Pine walked Notti back to the van, then walked over to kiss her son on each cheek,

"Your father would be so proud of you Professor Terence. I wish he could have seen you off."

"We'll give you a call when we get to Minnesota," said Mrs. Pine, showing her their map.

"And as soon as we get settled, we'll fly you out for a visit."

"Oh goodness I don't know if I need to get on a plane. That sounds awfully fancy. A bus ride will be fine, and then I can see all the other states along the way."

"We'll talk about it later, Mother. Now take good care of yourself and don't forget to call if you need anything."

"Goodbye Terence, drive safely," she said as tears fell from the pain f separation.

Quickly they pulled out onto the street. Notti watched her grandmother stand on the curb and wave as they drove away towards their new life.

Notti thought of how she had never been away from her grandma before. From the day she came home from the hospital, near her arms she always stayed. Over the years she learned many lessons. Like how to walk with her toes in front, instead of from side to side like a penguin.

How to properly chew her food. Forty chews per bite so doesn't work so hard to feed you.

Grandma always had a vegetable and a rose garden. Each beamed with beauty and bounty. Especially compared to her neighbor's yard, which stunk of garbage and junk everywhere.

Grandma's garden taught her how to appreciate vegetables, like tomatoes and green beans. When the tomatoes were ripe, she would drag the hose into the garden with a shaker of salt. With a quick spray of water and a dash of salt, she could eat to her heart's content.

Grandma taught her to sew, knit, can, and dry food to stock for the winter months.

Professor Pine shifted into fourth gear and drove the family up on to the highway. Suddenly everything familiar began to disappear, and the faster they drove, the more it all became a scenic blur of a place she always called home.

Chapter Three

TANGLE TOWN

Two days later Professor Pine downshifted into second gear and steered his family up ta hill and into their new neighborhood.

"Look, that must be Pratt Elementary school," said Mrs. Pine. She pointed to a large brick building with rows upon rows of white framed windows.

Notti thought the school looked old. With its empty playground and dried up lilac bushes it also looked sad. She tried to imagine what recess time would look like. Suddenly a mirage of the playground appeared to her.

Kids were dressed casually and playing hopscotch and dodge ball. Notti wondered what it would be like to not wear a uniform nor be taught by nuns. No Mother Superior to punish bad children with a slap of the ruler on the back of the hand. No Sister Pearl with her haunting stare and ill temper.

Notti knew this move had rescued her just in time from the Sister Victoria. The teacher who everyone knew didn't like children.

Notti then let out a happy sigh at the thought of Sister Sophie. The nicest teacher who always encouraged her to learn and to be kind.

Notti looked at her reflection in the car window.

She didn't like her permed straight hair. Nor the stupid white turtleneck shirt under the blue corduroy jumper. And not with the matching blue cable knit knee high socks. They made her feel too coordinated. Even down to her penny loafer shoes.

"Mom, do you think I'll fit in with the kids here? Will they think I'm different because I'm from the East Coast?"

"No, probably not much different. Off course you won't have that Midwestern nasal accent. Just don't engage in your excessive imagining and daydreaming and you'll be fine," said Mrs. Pine with a huff.

"You really don't want kids thinking you can see a giant coming out of a tree. Remember the time you scared those girls on the playground at Saint Monica school?"

Notti sank back into her seat and felt a pout emerging. The giant looked real. He hadn't said anything. She knew for some reason he wouldn't harm anyone. He merely carried a distressed squirrel from a dangling tree limb. And then placed him gently on the ground.

"It's not excessive," she whispered, thinking about how natural it was for her to imagine. Grandpa Pine taught her how to accept what she was given. Even if she didn't understand it. He reminded her that imagination was a gift to be celebrated and used, and not to be frightened of.

"What your mother is trying to say, is just keep your imaginative experiences to yourself. You're going into sixth grade now, so you're expected to be more mature," said her father.

"Fine," said Notti, rolling her eyes and sitting back up to get a better look at the neighborhood.

"Notti," scolded Mrs. Pine, while turning around to give Notti the "don't you dare talk back to your father" look. Notti looked away at a large oak tree across from the school that resembled an open umbrella. She lowered her eyes, and they rested on a sign in front of a stone church that read, "Happy Times Preschool."

"Oh look, that's where Rusty and Randy will go to preschool," said Mrs. Pine with a sigh. She felt quite cheerful to have a daycare in the neighborhood. Notti knew her mother would welcome relief from the twins and from their noise and mess. Also, from their constant time-outs for their annoying tantrums over the dumbest things. Things like, who got more brown sugar on their oatmeal, or who got to push the elevator door button first at the department store.

"Terence, look at that lovely English Tudor with the red door and the green groomed lawn," said Mrs. Pine.

"You're being redundant Annette. Lawns are typically green, especially if they're groomed," he said with a slight snort. Mrs. Pine rolled her eyes as if to dismiss his comment.

Notti noticed how every house looked so uniquely different. A large boxy brick house sat next to a small wooden cabin, and next to the cabin stood a tall gingerbread house with several stained-glass windows. A crooked brick path led up to a red plaid door with what looked like a white icing trim. She tried to imagine who would live in such a fun looking house. She decided it must be someone very special like a sweet grandmother.

Everyone's homes were adorned with flower beds and trimmed bushes, and the sidewalks meandered up and around like a narrow cement river. And there was no corner Italian grocery store with a submarine sandwich shop, or a penny candy window. This neighborhood was nothing like back home.

Mr. Pine turned onto another steep hill filled with cotton woods and maple trees.

"Look, it's a park with a pond and picnic tables," shouted Notti.

Everyone paused to look, and Notti thought briefly of the parks back home with bums napping on the benches and pigeon poop splattered everywhere. She felt filled with excitement at the idea of sitting on a park bench and reading her library books by the pond in peace and quiet. When they reached the top of the long hill, Mr. Pine braked to a complete stop.

"According to these directions, we're supposed to go straight," said Mrs. Pine, studying the realtor's map.

"What's the name of the street we're looking for?" asked Mr. Pine.

"Melrose," she said looking at the street that suddenly split into three different directions. They looked at each other and shrugged their shoulders. Mr. Pine rolled down the window and pointed his arm to the left.

"Let's go this way and see what's on the other side of this pond?"

Up another hill they chugged around the pond and the tennis court, and suddenly it appeared. Everyone watched a mysterious tall white tower with a black pointy roof appear.

Notti looked in awe at the many arched openings on the very top. She liked the way the tower looked as if it had come from a medieval fairy tale. Immediately, she imagined herself in the tower, overlooking the treetops and the roofs of all the homes, and within an instant she imagined herself there.

Standing inside the covered balcony of the tower, she could see the treetops and the roofs of the surrounding homes. The leaves were changing colors in slow motion. Changing from an array of green to yellow, to orange and finally to a brilliant red.

Suddenly the breeze lifted, and Notti imagined herself up into the sky. Her arms spread out as she prepared to fly over the roof tops of this beautiful neighborhood. The car engine let out a chug and a cough, and Notti fell like a sack of potatoes. She snapped out of her daydream with a jolt and found herself back in the seat just as Mr. Pine passed the tower.

The street turned sharply to the right, and then down a steep hill. Notti grabbed the car ceiling handles as her father took another sharp turn. She watched the tower disappear and giggled with delight at her brief imagined flight from its balcony.

"These streets are crazy. None of them go straight across," said Mrs. Pine as she turned the map upside-down again.

"We should be there Terrence. The address is 126 Melrose Street."

Mr. Pine nodded and drove a short straight stretch He turned right again, and then halfway up another hill into the driveway of a yellow house with dark shutters.

On the front steps sat a woman in her blue suit. When she saw the Pine family, she jumped up and came skipping to the passenger window. After patting her hair sprayed flip and straightening her skirt, she reached out her hand to greet Mrs. Pine.

"Hello, I'm Sally Hart from the realtor's office. Great timing, I just got here a few minutes ago. Welcome to Tower Hillside Park, or Tangle Town, which is what some people call it.

"That'an appropriate name for what we just drove through," said the Mr. Pine as he turned off the car engine.

Everyone piled out of the bus and into the house for an

introductory tour of their temporary furnished home.

Miss Heart explained to them how delighted Anderson's

were to not have to leave their home empty for a year while they

lived in England.

She then escorted Mrs. Pine through the living room and into the kitchen.

Mr. Pine quietly slipped out the side door to check on the backyard. Notti followed her mom and Miss Hart upstairs to inspect each room, And the boys sat down on the living room couch to watch the singing cowboy television show.

Casually, Mrs. Pine pointed to a bedroom and gestured to Notti with royal authority.

"This is your room Notti. Keep it clean and don't break what doesn't belong to you, or I'll put Randy in with you."

Notti shuddered at the thought, as she watched her mother strut down the hall with a slight bounce in her step. Curiously, Notti stepped into the small room and felt an instant relief that the window faced the backyard and not another house a few feet away. She sat on the full-size bed and lay back. She felt a nap coming on but quickly shook it off and went to retrieve her suitcase.

By evening everyone had unpacked and settled into a comfortable spot. Notti's stomach grumbled, so she wandered down to the kitchen. Mrs. Pine sat at the kitchen table emptying the cooler before deciding that there was nothing to eat for dinner.

"Terence, would you please go out and get a bucket of chicken with all the fixings?

Aand on your way home stop at the store for some ice cream and a bottle of chocolate syrup?"

"There's no such thing as some ice cream, Annette. You either want a pint, a half-gallon, or a gallon. Which is it?" he said from the living room.

"You decide Dear," she said rolling her eyes and shaking her head again. Surprised, Notti smiled at the idea of dessert.   She sauntered into the living room to see what was on television and whispered to herself, "I guess you're going off your diet again."

"What?" said Mrs. Pine?

"Oh nothing," said Notti while getting comfortable on the couch. It irritated her how Mom's diet meant no potato chips, French- fries or deserts for anyone, except on holidays and birthdays. Notti watched her father stand with his eyes glued to the nightly news cast, then grumble as he looked for his car keys.

Rusty and Randy screamed at each other over a plastic dinosaur, and Mr. Pine grumbled louder as he stepped over them.

"Stop it you two, or no ice cream," he scolded.

That's all it took, and they instantly stopped. Notti settled further into the cushions during this rare moment of silence, to think of all the scenes of the past couple of days.

Notti thought of the first night at the rustic motel in Ohio and listening to the hum of the highway. She thought of the next morning leaving in the dark and driving by acres of farms until they saw the skyscrapers of Chicago. When they crossed the Mississippi River into Minnesota, her father talked about the land of ten thousand lakes that were made from glaciers. Of the native people who came from the east and harvested wild rice into their canoes. Notti thought of Grandma Pine's stories of living on the reservation as a child, and of her Dutch and African American father, and his Native American mother. They had made the decision to move to the city for work, and once her great grandpa found a job they never went back. Notti wondered if there would be other mixed kids like her in Tangle Town.

Mr. Pine left for the store and soon returned with his arms full of bags and a bucket of fried chicken. Mrs. Pine gave Notti her typical stern look, which meant to set the table. She handed her the bag of paper plates and utensils. Notti set the table with still hopes of one day earning an allowance. She didn't want to have to ask for change to buy a candy bar or a comic book. She hoped Mom would let her take neighborhood babysitting jobs soon. And where she could charge by the hour and make some real money.

When everyone was seated, Mrs. Pine entered, carrying the bucket of chicken and a pair of tongs. She gave herself the largest breast, her husband the smaller one, the twins each got a leg, and Notti a thigh.

"One day I'll get a job and buy my own chicken. I'll give myself the breast instead of this boney thigh," thought Notti with a frown.

Mrs. Pine served the mashed potatoes and corn to everyone before sitting down to take her first large bite. As she chewed, she licked her fingers in-between bites. Notti thought of how Mom really liked her chicken and how she made eating it look so delicious.

Soon after ice cream and chocolate syrup, a very tired family climbed the stairs to bed. Feeling the evening chill, Notti kept her robe on over her nightgown and dove in under the covers. The new room with its new sounds suddenly haunted her. She listened, wondering if there were thieves on the streets of quiet neighborhoods.

Back home, she recalled the day when a robber ran from the police. He leaped over her grandparents' fence into the yard. The police caught the robber and held him at gun point.

Notti watched from an upstairs window. Grandma yelled for her to get away from the window. Grandpa locked all the doors and told everyone to get down. The memory made her tremble as she listened to the faint murmurs of this new neighborhood.

Within the darkness she suddenly remembered Grandma's words of think of your grandpa before you go to sleep. Notti relaxed and remembered when Grandpa used to read stories to her about sailors and pirate ships. She couldn't imagine what it must have been like to be shipwrecked on an island. Or to be discovered by pirates. She thought of Grandpa's baritone voice and the drama and excitement he brought to every word.

"I miss you," she whispered as her eyelids soon relaxed and slowly shut for the night. In her dream came a distant and familiar faint cry of seagulls and the crashing of waves upon a shore.

Chapter Four

THE PIRATE DREAM

Notti stirred and sat up with a sudden jolt. She looked around through squinted eyes for anything to focus on. The morning sun rose to warm her face. She searched beyond the shrieking seagulls sailing on the gentle high winds.

"Notti," said a hushed voice. She turned and found to her surprise, Grandpa Pine kneeling behind her.

"Hide this," he said, shoving something into her robe pocket before taking her hand.

"And next time you think of me, don't think of pirates or anything dangerous."

"What, where am I?"

"Notti dearest, you're on my ship."

"What ship?"

"The North Star and we're under attack."

A mounting swell splashed over the stern and drenched Notti and Grandpa Pine. Notti screamed and rubbed the salt water from her burning eyes. Suddenly she heard a booming voice as loud as a megaphone. It forced her eyes to open wider in to see Grandpa Pine yanked away.

"Where's the gold? Tell me or you're a dead man," said a pirate.

He stood like a giant and held Grandpa by the neck with one hand. The pirate pointed a pistol to Grandpa's chest with the other hand.

"Grandpa," cried Notti, as she rushed to him. She reached for his jacket just as two monstrous hands grabbed and threw her up in the air. She flew from one ship to another like a hooked fish and landed onboard the slick wet floor.

"Let my granddaughter go! There's no gold! I am a simple merchant," shouted Grandpa Pine. The giant pirate gripped his neck even tighter. Notti screamed and rolled across the deck. Another swell plummeted over her, and again, the salt water burned her eyes. She forced them open. Only this time to see the flapping of a black flag with an emblem of skull and crossbones. Her heart raced as her gaze lowered to a scraggly crew of men rushing to her feet.

"Pick her up you mangy thieves," commanded the giant's demanding voice.

"Aye, aye Captain Howell," muttered two other pirates. They pulled Notti up as she struggled to turn to see her grandpa.

"I have no more time for your lies," yelled the giant within inches of Grandpa Pine's face.

"Don't look Notti," cried Grandpa. The giant pulled the trigger, and the sound of the shot rang through Notti and shook her uncontrollably. With weakened knees, she slumped over while the pirates held up her trembling body. They dragged her to the top of a stairwell. Notti could hear heavy stomping. And within seconds a rotting odor breathed on her neck. A forceful hand then clutched her haggard hair.

"Get down those stairs," hissed the giant with quivering soiled white sideburns. His snot filled hairy nostrils flared with every breath. He pushed her down the steps. She tumbled in what felt like slow motion over each step. One at a time it impacted her body with a sharp pain. A cabin door suddenly appeared, and she sailed through it. She landed with a thud on her hands and knees. The door slammed shut and locked behind her.

Notti stood up in the darkness and rubbed her bruised arms and legs. She bent over and coughed out a foul smell. Quickly, she covered her mouth and swallowed hard to keep from vomiting. The ship rocked and swayed. Her eyes finally adjusted, and she found a large barrel to hold on to. Her heart pounded like the heavy beat of a conga drum, and her tears began to flow and puddle on her chin. A stream of light caught her eye. With a sense of hope she made her way around large filled sacks and many barrels. Something jabbed her thigh, and when she reached down to rub it, her hand brushed against her robe pocket.

In the dim light. she pulled out and opened a small drawstring bag full of colorful gems. She wondered why Grandpa had given it to her.

"Surely the pirates were looking for gold coins or bars, and not gems", she whispered.

Tripping over shadowy forms, she moved cautiously once again toward the light. As she drew closer, she could see the light emitting from under a door. A resonating murmur grew louder. She peered through a wide keyhole to see three pirates sitting on barrels around a large crate. They argued amongst themselves in a cloud of tobacco smoke.

"He did it again and believe me this is the last time we take a ship with nothing worth stealing," growled a toothless pirate.

"Yeah Mick, and he calls himself a captain."

"I'm telling you Joe, shooting that old man before he coughed up the gold, ain't' nothin' but stupid," complained Mick with his long greasy mustache. Notti shuddered and bit her lip to hold in her anger.

"Yeah Joe, and even if he did have any gold we'll never know unless we tear the whole ship apart," said a bald one with a large tattoo of a whale on his arm.

"I say we take this ship before we reach the coast and dock at Port Sun Beach," sneered Joe.

"No, let the quartermaster decide. He'll know when to seize her, "said Mick while twisting the end of his moustache. "When we're rid of the captain, we should set sail to the west side of Africa where the gold is," squealed Joe.

His gold ring earrings dangled and clanked together like chimes catching the breeze. Mick lowered his voice.

"It's been said by the mates on deck, that when we reach the mouth of the Biri Biri river, we're to follow quartermaster Low and the captain to a pub. Low would be challenging him to a drinking contest and fool him by sucking down a bottle of water instead. Do you see what I'm saying'? Captain drinks and drinks, and Low pays a married woman t o hang all over the captain. The husband comes in and bam, out goes Captain, and off with the ship we go."

Everyone nodded and Joe let out a satisfying chuckle. The door suddenly opened and alarmed the men to their feet. They reached for their knives just as an anxious boy came running in.

"What do you want?" growled Joe.

"Master Low said the loot is on board and Captain Howell is ready to lift anchor. He said we have sugar, hides and tobacco."

Not able to hold it in any longer, Notti banged her fists on the door and screamed.

"You'll pay for this you wicked thieves and murders."

The boy watched the pirates climb the stairs, laughing and unmarred by Notti's curse. As soon as they were gone, the boy pulled from his pocket a ring of keys and hurried to the storage door.

"What's your name?" he asked in a gentle voice.

"I'm Notti, who are you?"

"I'm Patrick the cabin boy," he said fiddling with the key. She heard a loud clank, and the door opened.

"Come on, there's a mutiny coming, and this might be my only chance to get off this ship and get back home to Ireland. Just like you, the captain stole me from my papa's ship and forced me to work for him. Once the captain's gone, we can get to shore, hide, and wait for help.

Notti came out of the storage room to stand slightly shorter than Patrick. Through the dirt and grime, she could see his fair skin and red locks of hair. He nervously batted his lashes over his deep green eyes and licked his sun cracked lips.

"They shot him," she blurted out as the tears returned and her body trembled uncontrollably."

"I'm sorry. They're evil men, so come on, and I'll help you get out of here."

They felt the ship turn, and Patrick grabbed her hand as Notti wiped her tears away.

"Hurry," he said running up the narrow and slippery stairs. Notti lifted her nightgown to keep from tripping and climbed up after him. When they reached the top step, Patrick cautiously opened the door. He stuck his head out before signaling to Notti. Together they dashed behind a row of water barrels. They crouched down when they heard a piercing whistle. They peeked above the barrels as the crew and Captain Howell directed the ship towards the river. He shouted his orders and paused, then giddily sang to himself. His stomach jiggled and hung over his pants. He paced back and forth in joyful anticipation of a day out on the town. The anchor finally dropped, and Quartermaster

Low, Sailing Master Joe, Helmsman Ricky, and Captain Howell climbed into the large rowing dinghy.

With his unshaven face and cocky grin, the captain sat back comfortably to enjoy the silent ride down river. The aging helmsman huffed and strained with each pull of the paddle to keep the boat straight. Captain Howell turned to observe the retreating sea. Patrick and Notti nervously crouched lower to avoid his gaze as they waited for their moment of escape.

Notti could feel the weight of tension from the remaining crew. They gallivanted around the ship doing their chores and repairs. They pretended not to look at the captain. The caulker sang as he poured hot pitch into the gaps to keep the ship watertight. The deck mates worked on the bilge water pumps to draw up the stinking water from the ship.

The dingy finally reached the shore, and everyone but the helmsman climbed out. They all trudged through the shallow waters. Once on shore, Captain Howell led the way. He gleefully strolled toward the neighboring village.

On board, Notti listened to the crying seagulls as the sea breeze echoed a calm hum. The helmsman returned to the ship. He was visibly exhausted with sweat running and pooling all over him. With great effort, he climbed the rope ladder. He joined the crew in the main cabin to wait for Low and his mates to return.

Patrick signaled to Notti with a nudge that this was their chance. He pointed to the hanging rope ladder and together they ran for the stern. Climbing over the railing, he reached for the rope and climbed down.

"We're going to have to jump and swim, so stay close," he called up in a loud whisper. Balancing himself at the end of the ladder like a trapeze artist, he gave Notti a reassuring look. Then he jumped in with a minimal splash.

Notti grabbed the rope, pulled her night gown up above her knees and managed somehow to climb down. For a second, she looked at the water with much uncertainty and felt stuck. Clinging to the rope like a lifeline, she thought of what if no one found them and they never got home?

Notti put her arms and legs into motion. But no matter how hard she kicked and stroked, the current pulled even harder. Down she went with a mouthful of brine water, and up she surfaced struggling to breathe. She coughed and gagged as more water rushed into her mouth and nose.

"Notti, Notti, cried Patrick. Where are you?" She heard him once, then twice, before she went under one last time.

Chapter Five

HATTLY ELEMENTARY

The wind whipped across the window and rattled the pane like a drum roll. Notti's eyes flew open into the darkness of her bedroom. Cold and wet she shivered, and for a moment she

felt panicked thinking she had wet the bed.

Suddenly, the memory of the escape filled her thoughts. A flash of light surged through the window and struck the floor. It fizzled like a lit firecracker, spouting fiery droplets in every direction. Notti gasped, and before she could decide what to do, the droplets rapidly grew and from each emerged a portion of her entire dream.

Patrick swam towards her while the pirate ship sailed through the window and into the night. Notti's pounding heart echoed with fear. She watched the foot of her bed turn into a large rock with small waves crashing over it. She leaped up and ran to the door. She turned to see the dream fill her room with the rush of water covering everything in its path.

"Oh no," stammered Notti, trying not to scream while she leaned up against the door. As the water progressed, she felt for and found the doorknob. She turned it and the door opened seconds before her room disappeared into the rising water. Down the hallway she ran, and the dream followed. It spread and filled every nook and crevice with the speed of poured maple syrup. Patrick continued to swim towards something up. and holding. There were no words, but she could read his lips calling her name over and over as she ran backwards down the hall. Tripping over her own feet she fell back into the bathroom and rushed to shut the door. She watched the river creep underneath the door, and another surge of panic shot through her.

"I'll be trapped and drown in the bathroom," she said.

The dream seeped through the hinges and flowed in so quickly that the water was already up to her ankles. Trembling, she brushed up against the wall and over the light switch. The light flicked on and suddenly the dream vanished.   Though stunned, Notti let out a sigh of relief as she backed up to the toilet and sat on the lid.

"The dream was so real," she whispered, thinking of Grandpa, the pirate ship, and Patrick. Slowly and with caution she got up and opened the door to an empty hall. Listening, she could hear her father snoring and a gentle breeze rapping against the windows. She shook her head with uncertainty. And couldn't fathom how her imagination could make a river flow into a room, and a pirate ship sail through a window.

"How did I dream that?"

Throwing off her wet robe and night gown into the bathtub, she grabbed a towel and wrapped it around herself. Sitting back down on the toilet lid, she pondered the how's and whys. Of the most vivid and realistic dream she had ever experienced. This was nothing like her daydreaming or imagining.

Feeling a bit chilled, she knew she couldn't sit and think about it all night. Morning would mean school, and she wanted to be rested for her first day. Slowly she stood and reached for the bathroom light switch. But then she drew her hand back, fearing the dream might return. Tiptoeing back to her room, she kicked something and watched it slide across the floor.

"It's the bag of gems," she whispered picking it up with wonder. She took a closer look at her bracelet. It held one gem and several empty bezels where maybe other gems had once set. She wondered what the other gems could do. Notti imagined how beautiful her bracelet would look filled with more gems.

"It would look like a real piece of jewelry," she whispered as she put the gems into her jewelry box.

"I need to find another nightgown to wear, because if Mom finds the one, I'm wearing, I'll have to tell her about my dreamtime."

In the laundry room she found another nightgown and threw the wet one into the dryer to dry. Back up the stairs she flew into her room and quietly slipped under the covers. She thought of Patrick and how he helped her to escape from the pirates, and she wondered and hoped he had found his way back to Ireland. Going over the dream again and again while tapping her finger on the bracelet, she listened to the crickets. She yawned long and hard. Shortly afterwards her head nodded once, twice, and on the third nod she fell asleep. And the dreamtime bracelet shimmered in the light of an almost full moon.

****

"Notti are you up?" called Mrs. Pine from the kitchen. "Notti get up!"

Notti opened her eyes and quickly squinted at the morning light. Sitting up, she scanned her room. No pirate ship, no river, and no Patrick. just the nightstand with the funky beaded lamp that someone must have made at summer camp. The antique dresser drawers sat open and filled with her clothes. on the rocker sat her stuffed horse with the missing eye, the torn hoof, and the stuffing hanging from the left hind leg.

Notti relaxed back into her pillow, and relieved that the dream hadn't returned. Casually, she glanced at the clock and sat up in an instant. She realized that her first day of school would begin in forty-four minutes.

"Oh no," she said leaping out of bed. Something on her wrist moved and for a moment she felt suspended in space. It was as if all her senses were suddenly heightened. She could smell the air, hear the leaves outside her window, and see the pores on the top of her hand.

"It's the bracelet," she whispered, touching it gently.

"Notti, are you up and getting ready? I'll drive you in," called her mother with an impatient tone. Notti ran to the dresser and found her under clothes, a corduroy skirt, a long sleeve flannel top, and a pair of knee-high socks. She scrambled into them. She took a moment in front of the mirror to frown at her slightly knocked knees and uncurled hair. Hurrying into the bathroom, she splashed her face with warm water and pulled her crazed hair back into a ponytail with a red hair tie. Having purposely forgotten the tortuous curlers, she knew her hair would not go unnoticed by her mother's inspection. She didn't care. Last night had been strange enough without having to sleep with her head in painful curlers.

Bounding down the first three steps, she looked to see if anyone was looking, then jumped on the railing and slid the rest of the way down on her bottom. Landing quietly on her feet, she sauntered into the kitchen pretending she had plenty of time.

Mrs. Pine sat drinking her black coffee and reading the newspaper. She looked up and scanned Notti from head to toe with her usual critical eye.

"Why don't you wear that nice red plaid skirt I got for you and with the blue turtle-neck sweater?"

Notti rolled her eyes, grabbed a delicious red apple, her lunch box and her backpack.

"Why can't I get you to eat anything?" continued her mother while standing and pointing to the box of cereal as she followed her out the door to the garage.

Notti zipped up her jacket as the air stirred briskly with the first hints of Fall. They hurried into the van and Mrs. Pine slowly backed out of the garage. Ever since she backed out of a parking space and accidentally almost knocked over an old lady, she always inched her way out. The woman had explained to Mrs. Pine how she only experienced a bruised knee. Mrs claimed it was her own fault for being on the driver's blind side.

Mr. Pine said he had never heard of a person apologizing for being the cause of an accident. Notti held back a giggle as she watched her mother safely pull out of the driveway.

"Where's Dad?"

"He walked the twins to preschool, and then walked to the university," said Mrs. Pine.

"Oh, that's great that he can walk to work," said Notti looking out at her quiet new neighborhood.

"Yes, well you know how your father likes to walk. He'll most likely walk every day," she said with a sigh as they drove by the water tower.

Notti looked up at the tower and suddenly felt a twinge in her stomach. She quickly shifted her gaze toward the approaching school as Mrs. Pine cruised down the hill and into the school parking lot. Notti rubbed her tummy and took a deep breath.

"Now I'll pick you up right here, so have a good day, and don't worry, you'll be fine," said Mrs. Pine while giving her a reassuring glance.

Notti jumped out and walked to the sounds of laughter. Soon the playground came into view, and she felt her heart skip a beat as she stepped in.

"Watch out," cried a lanky boy as a ball came whizzing toward Notti's head. She caught the ball inches from her face and threw it back.

"Hey, good catch, thanks," said the boy running back to his game.

Notti looked around to see much activity. Mostly, boys playing dodge ball and girls jumping rope or playing hopscotch.

"Hi," said a tall girl, as she flipped her long blonde hair off her shoulders.

"Hi," said Notti, marveling at how blonde her hair looked. She had seen dirty blonde, strawberry blonde, but never almost white, blonde.

"Do you want to jump rope with us?" asked the girl while pointing to the other girl.

"Sure," said Notti, placing the backpack on the steps and following the girl to a corner near the fence

"My name is Amity, and this is Hanna." Hanna picked up one end of the rope and together she and Amy whipped the rope around like two cowgirls about to lasso a calf.

"Jump in," roared Amity. Notti rocked back and forth, counting one, two, three, and four, then saw an opening and jumped in. Notti lifted herself with ease into the air. The fear of the unknown and of a new grade and a new neighborhood suddenly disappeared. Amity recited a rhyme and turned the rope faster and faster.

Grasping the rhythm, Notti felt her body moving in slow motion, and even the rope slowed, as time also seemed to slow down. The rhyme echoed in her ears as she laughed out loud and suddenly felt good about being in Tangle Town.

A piercing ring brought the rope to a stop, and Hanna and Amity ran for their backpacks.

"See you at recess," shouted Hanna.

Notti watched as the playground emptied, and the stairs filled with orderly chaos. Lines formed and students raced up the stairs through the gray double doors. Notti picked up her backpack and followed behind, remembering how at St. Monica, the teachers would never allow racing. Instead, students would get into lines with no running, and no talking, laughing, nor shouting.

Notti climbed up the second set of stairs with the rest of the kids who poured into the stairwell. She found room 203 and took one last deep breath before letting it out. Slowly, she entered the classroom to begin her new school life.

"I redid your seating assignments, so look for your name on top of your desk and sit down so I can take attendance." Said a tall man with a greased down mustache, curly hair, and a small red bow tie. Notti blinked, and for a moment he looked like a pirate from her dream.

"You must be Notti," he said with a nod and a smile, showing a full set of extra white teeth.

"Yes, I am," said Notti with a curious smile.

"Well, welcome, I'm your teacher Mr. Johnson," he said with a look of pride as he fiddled with his bow tie.

"Now find your desk so we can get started."

Notti moved in between the rows looking for her desk. She didn't look at anyone. As soon as she saw her name she sat down. To her left she saw the name Jake. When she looked up, there he was with half opened sleepy eyes and his finger digging up in his nose. He pulled out the biggest and greenest booger Notti had ever seen. He then quickly popped it into his mouth and swallowed it down.

"That one tasted like lime," he said with a look of surprise.

Disgusted, Notti looked away at the desk on her right. It read Hanna. She looked up into the dark eyes of her new jump rope partner.

"Hi again, my whole name is Hanna McDonald," she said with a giggle.

"Hi, my name is Notti Pine," said Notti with also a giggle.

"Wow, you're named after a tree, that's really cool," said Hanna with a nod of approval.

"Attention everyone, let's get started," said Mr. Johnson. He looked at his watch, played with his tie, and repeatedly nodded his head. The bell rang again, and Notti looked around curiously.

"That's the tardy bell," whispered Hanna.

"Oh, in my old school Father Burke rang the tardy chime," whispered Notti.

"Hmm, that's different," said Hanna, though she couldn't imagine a chime working here.

"Well, if you come in after the bell, you have to go to the office and get a tardy slip from the wicked witch of the hill," said Hanna.

"She's a witch?"

"She's just really unfriendly and angry looking."

"Oh," said Notti, knowing now to never to be tardy.

The door opened and a boy ran in with his head down and his baseball cap pulled over his eyebrows. He slid into his chair in front of Notti, and took off his cap. Out popped a bundle of small locks and curls. Curiously, Notti sensed a need to touch them, but as she reached for one curl in particular, the boy turned around. It was as if he knew someone was looking at him. Notti's mouth immediately dropped open, as she stood to see the name on his desk.

"Patrick?" she blurted out, reading his name tag.

"Hi," said Patrick with blushed cheeks.

"Is there something you want, Notti?" asked Mr. Johnson looking at the name tag on her desk.

"Oh no". said Notti, sitting back down.

Patrick turned back around. The class all watched Mr. Johnson adjust his tie and check his watch several more times. Notti sat embarrassed and stunned with a blank stare.   She wondered what everyone must be thinking about her outburst.

"Hey, who's the new girl?" squealed a voice from the back row. Notti turned around to see a portly brown boy with a large round nose. He sat with his chair leaning back against the wall.

He grinned at Notti with his eyes bugged out like a frog.

"Set your chair down Kelly," insisted Mr. Johnson. Kelly leaned forward slightly and pouted.

"Class, this is Notti Pine, and she comes to our school from the east coast state of Connecticut. For those of you who don't. remember where that is, it's right here."

He pointed to the upper right corner of a large map hanging behind his desk.

"At recess you may all introduce yourselves to her if you'd like," he concluded with an air of arrogance. Mr. Johnson continued to talk and give out instructions. Notti didn't hear a word as she continued to sit in shock behind Patrick. A loud crash turned everyone around to see Kelly on the floor. His legs were up in the air and his chair was turned over. The class roared with laughter while Kelly picked up his chair and bowed.

"He's the class clown and will do anything for attention," said Hanna. as She dug inside her desk. "Take out your math book."

"Oh," said Notti.
"Are you okay Notti?" Notti nodded and leaned over to whisper.
"Yeah, I just don't remember where I saw Patrick before. I must have met him somewhere or I wouldn't have had a dream about him."
Hanna's mouth dropped open.

"You've never seen him before, and you dreamt about him?"

"Yes," whispered Notti as she dug out her book.
"I hear whispering when it should be quiet," said Mr. Johnson as his eyes scanned the classroom. Hanna and Notti opened their books and Notti rolled her eyes, wishing she had kept her mouth shut about Patrick.

"Okay, let's begin with chapter two and the word equations," said Mr. Johnson. He kept an eye on Kelly, a hand on his tie, and a jiggle of his head to shake off his annoyance.

Time passed unusually fast. Notti was thankful that Mr. Johnson had kept them busy with math problems and reading assignments. When the recess bell finally rang, everyone lined up by the door. Notti looked at Patrick wishing she knew what to say.

She thought of casually saying something like "oh, by the way, were you swimming in my bedroom last night?" Or "did you happen to drop a bracelet in my hallway?"

'He'll think I'm crazy, or making it up just to get his attention," she thought. The more she thought about it the more she decided to just drop it.

Mr. Johnson led the class down the hallway with a sternness that meant business.

"No pushing, no fighting, and no leaving the playground whatsoever. Is that clear?"

"Yes, Mr. Johnson," everyone recited as they filed out into the autumn air. They grabbed jump ropes, hula hoops and dodge balls.

Notti followed Hanna to the hopscotch court where Amity was already playing with another girl. Amity introduced Notti to her friend Kay before taking a turn. Notti, Hanna, and Kay all watched and waited by the fence.

Chapter Six

CROWS AND MESSAGES

"I've been waiting all through math to ask what kind of dream you had about Patrick," asked Hanna.

Notti looked at Hanna's inquisitive eyes and hesitated. She didn't know where to begin, or how to tell her.

"Was it scary?" continued Hanna with a frown.

Kay played hopscotch and threw the pebble then hopped from number to number. Amity ran off to the drinking fountain.

"Yes," blurted out Notti, while still feeling embarrassed.

"It's strange because I'm on a pirate ship trying to escape and Patrick is helping me. When I wake up, the dream follows me into my room."

Notti looked at Hanna's reaction and wondered if she thought she was making it up.

"Wow! What happened to Patrick?" asked Hanna with a surge of enthusiasm.

Feeling a little more confident, Notti continued.

"He swam into my room holding my bag of my bracelet gems," said Notti pulling up the sleeve of her jacket.

"Double wow," said Hanna with her eyes bugged out.

Notti pulled her sleeve down just as Amity returned. Notti and Hanna listened to her complaints about their teacher, Mr. Johnson.

"Did you see the way he kept playing with his tie and bobbing his head? I think he's nervous, or kind of goofy," said Amity.

"'Definitely goofy," said Hanna. Notti agreed and pretended to be listening, but her thoughts were elsewhere. Hanna handed over the pebble to Notti, who stepped up to take her turn. A crow flew by making a familiar caw. It was followed by four more crows who circled above Notti's head. Alarmed, Notti crouched down thinking they were going to attack. They continued to caw at her from a few feet away. Everyone standing nearby gathered to watch the bird spectacle with spontaneous oohs and aahs.

"They're going to attack her," yelled a boy from the crowd. The crows stopped circling and rose in unison to form a straight line. Cawing louder, they flew toward Notti as she threw up her hands to protect herself. They missed her and darted around a tree before flying down the street. The crows didn't return, and just as quickly as it had all begun, it ended. Notti stood paralyzed in shock. Everyone else shrugged it off and went back to playing.

"Whoa, did you see that?" asked Hanna.
"Of course, we saw it," said Amity.
Hanna ran up to Notti. "Are you okay?"
"Sure, yeah, I'm fine," answered Notti, still puzzled.
"Don't worry, I had crows fly over me once. My aunt Lizzy said that crows are a good sign," continued Hanna.

"A good sign for what?" asked Notti, somewhat flustered as she gripped the pebble.

"She says, they're messengers, and that their caw is usually a warning of some kind. Like something important will happen and you'll learn from it."

"You mean I'm going to learn something in school?" asked Notti, still confused.

"No, you're going to learn something about yourself that will change you."

"Oh! How does your aunt know that?"

"She's a naturalist, and she works with animals and birds. She's always telling me about what birds can do. Maybe you can meet her sometime."

Amity tapped Notti on the shoulder. "You're holding up the game," she said with her hand out. Notti dropped the pebble onto her hand before sitting down on the steps next to Hanna.

"Tell me again why crows want to warn me?"

"My aunt says they're smarter than we think, and they can see things we can't."

"What kind of things?"

The recess bell rang, and Hanna and Notti stood aside to let the crowd of students stampede by.

"I don't know, but we could ask her. She lives across from the Witch's Tower. Do you want to meet her?" Notti's' eyes lit up as she and Hanna fell into line behind everyone else. They marched up the stairs instead of racing up them like everyone else.

"The Witch's Tower, what are you talking about?"

"The water tower, silly; it's called the Witch's Tower because the roof is dark and pointy like a witch's hat," said Hanna.

"Oh," said Notti, as they found their desks and slipped into their seats.

"Alright class, now take out your history books and a sheet of notebook paper," ordered   Mr. Johnson. He looked through his glasses sitting at the end of his nose and scanned the room to make sure everyone was listening.

"Now turn to page twenty-three, and let's begin with the American Civil War," he said with a haunting stare.

"Ugh," whispered Notti as she dug out her book and ripped out a sheet of notebook paper. We're probably going to talk about slaves now, she thought rolling her eyes. Notti secretly wished that American history wasn't always about slavery. She remembered a novel on slavery and the civil war, and the disgust she felt over the brutality and pain the characters had endured.

"Well?" said Hanna, nudging Notti.

Notti snapped out of her thoughts and looked curiously at Hanna.

"Well, what?"
"Do you want to meet my Aunt Lizzy or not?"
 "Sure," said Notti while quickly remembering why.
"Good, I'll meet you out front after the last bell."

"Why do I hear whispering?" asked Mr. Johnson as he scribbled the reading assignment on the board. Notti opened her history book while Mr. Johnson engaged in all his goofy nervous habits. Including a new one where he tapped his chin with his finger, over, and over again.

In her book there were pictures of Africans half naked standing on an auction block. And men in colonial garb stood in front of a crowd. Mr. Johnson read and commented on the sale of slaves, and Notti shuddered and kept her eyes on the text. She wondered if any of her classmates except for Kelly were looking to see her reaction.

"Why can't we learn about the African people before they came to America?" She thought. *"They had lives and work, and maybe a really interesting history."*

Fidgeting in her chair, she tried to imagine who the Africans were before they were shipped to America. Notti looked up in time to see the entire class with their heads buried in their books suddenly fade away. A dark mist appeared and settled while a flame emerged expanding into a campfire. Notti found herself sitting around the blaze listening to a village storyteller recite a tale about the jungle. Villagers gathered around to listen and to watch closely the storyteller's facial expressions and dramatic hand gestures. He described the gigantic water-laden trees, the sound of the trumpeting elephants, and the many chattering monkeys. To Notti, the villagers appeared to be Pygmies or Bushmen with beautiful round heads and peppercorn clusters of hair. No one seemed to take any notice of Notti. They were all thoroughly engaged in the story. They let out a cheer as the storyteller stood and thrust his hand into the air.

"This, the Turi, this is our forest!"

With those final words, the villagers and the campfire disappeared. Notti found herself back in the classroom with Mr. Johnson spewing orders about their homework assignment.

"Answer the ten topic questions and be prepared for a pop quiz on Thursday," he concluded with a wave of his hand. Notti sighed, wishing she could have stayed around the campfire to learn more about the Turi rainforest. Hanna looked curiously at Notti's glazed eyes but said nothing as she wrote down the history   assignment.

The day progressed at an even pace. Lunch in the cafeteria proved to be a nice change from the classroom. Notti joined Hanna, Kay, and Amity at their table. Notti noticed Patrick sitting with a few other boys from another class. She did her best to avoid any eye contact with him. After lunch, the afternoon moved at a slower pace but finally ended with spelling before the final bell rang. Notti packed up her backpack, and from the corner of her eye she watched Patrick fill his backpack too. Out of the blue he turned and stared shyly as if searching for the right words.

"I have an extra issue of Mu Land, if you'd like to have it," he said handing over his magazine with a sincere smile.

"Oh sure, what's it about?" asked Notti looking at the cover picture of a large lizard sitting under a palm tree.

"It's a comic book about a lost land and the adventures of the people who live there."

"Come on Patrick, Scouts starts in five minutes," said a boy waiting by the door.

"Okay Cody, I'm coming. Notti, I thought you might like this. I like to read and learn about ancient people and lands. Someday I hope to travel to different places. See you later Notti."

"

"Bye, and thanks," said Notti flipping through the pages. She stopped and held in a small gasp. Her eyes caught the picture of a man who looked just like the storyteller from her daydream. His hands were raised while he spoke to everyone seated around him. Notti looked up wanting to ask Patrick how he knew, but he had already left.

"Wow," she said, packing the magazine away and hurrying out the door. Hanna was waiting for her on the front steps, and so was Notti's mother.

"Hi Notti, did you have a good day?"

"Hi Mom, yeah it was okay, and this is Hanna," she said pointing to her new friend.

"Hello Hanna, I'm Mrs. Pine."

"Hi," said Hanna shyly.

"May I go with Hanna to her aunt's house for a little bit? She lives up by the tower."

Mrs. Pine raised her eyebrows questionably at first but then smiled and nodded.

"Give me your aunt's address Hanna. Notti' I'll phone your father and have him pick you up on his way home."

"Okay, it's 1144 Tower Ave," said Hanna.

"Good, now you two have a nice visit. And Notti, you'll have less than an hour before Dad picks you up."

Mrs. Pine drove off, and Hanna and Notti began their trek up the hill. When they reached the pond, Notti stopped to look at her reflection. A gentle breeze kicked up the leaves and sent them dancing around her. Hanna adjusted her pack, and in an instant a golden ray of light appeared around them both. Notti turned to look at Hanna. "Do you see that?"

"See what?" asked Hanna while tightening the strap on her bag.
"That light," said Notti, pointing to their reflection.
"What light? I don't see anything"
"You don't see it? It's all around us."
"Nope, but if you see it, I believe you. Aunt Lizzy says lots of people can see things like auras and energy fields and stuff. You can ask her about that too. Come on let's go."

Notti watched the light fade away and finally disappear. She sighed deeply, shook her head, and caught up to Hanna.

"Ever since I got here, strange things keep happening," said Notti as she followed Hanna.

"You mean like your dream and the crows?"

"Yeah," replied Notti as they came near the tower.

Notti stopped and felt a sudden shift in her balance. A heightened sensation came over her. She felt as if she were being lifted from the ground. When she looked down, there were her feet still firmly planted.

"What's the matter?" asked Hanna, realizing Notti had stopped again.
"I don't know. I feel light, like I'm being lifted. But I can't be because I'm standing here."
"Wow! Well, come on, we're almost there, that's her house," she said pointing to the cedar gingerbread cottage with a little

red door. Notti remembered wondering who lived there when they first drove through the neighborhood. Hanna was already on the brick path, so Notti hurried across the street, and up to the front door. Hanna pressed the doorbell, and a beautiful chime filtered through the keyhole.

"Aunt Lizzy, it's me Hanna," she shouted, ringing the bell again. They heard footsteps followed by a silent pause. The door opened to the rosy cheeked smile of a petite woman with curly white hair and dressed in a long dark tunic.

Chapter Seven

AUNT LIZZY

"Hello Hanna. Welcome, welcome and come right on in," she said. While wrapping her arms around her niece and squeezing her like a favorite teddy bear. Hanna blushed and Aunt Lizzy showered her with loud kisses.

"How's my girl on this fabulous, fine day?"

"I'm okay. This is my friend Notti," said Hanna while gently maneuvering out of Aunt Lizzy's loving grip.

"She just moved here from the east coast and strange things keep happening to her. I thought maybe you could help her." Aunt Lizzy looked at Notti up and down, smiled, and reached out her hand.

"Hello Notti, and welcome to the neighborhood."

"Hello Miss," said Notti admiring Aunt Lizzy's colorful enamel bracelets.

"Oh, you can call me Lizzy, that's what people have called me in all of my lives."

Notti didn't bother to ask what she meant by that. She did noticed Hanna taking off her shoes and setting them on a shelf by the door.

"It's customary in our family to leave the outside dirt and debris by the door," said Aunt Lizzy with a chuckle. Notti took off her shoes but hoped she had worn socks without holes in the toes. She checked her toes and sighed with relief.

"Let's go into the kitchen and see if I can find you two a snack after your long day at school."

Aunt Lizzy bounced through the house like a happy puppy with Hanna and Notti following close behind. They passed by large colorful paintings of birds and butterflies in flower gardens, and woodland animals in the forest. Patchwork quilts and lace doilies draped over the backs of the couch and stuffed chairs. And beautiful, lush houseplants nestled near every window. In another room, books piled high in stacks on the floor and in large bookcases. Notti's eyes caught the jacket of one book on her desk, titled Mu Land Uncovered. She couldn't help but wonder if it was a coincidence to see the same name of a place she had never heard of before twice in one day. Aunt Lizzy glanced back at Notti, and for a second their eyes locked.

"I'm doing a lot of research on the relationship of man, animals, and the natural world," said Lizzy, gesturing with modesty at her organized mess.

"I'm studying an indigenous clan from the south pacific who practiced a unique relationship with nature. They could take on the physical and mental characteristics of animals, and they could also communicate with the weather."

"Wow, that's amazing," said Notti, not knowing what else to say.
"Yes, indeed it is," said Aunt Lizzy as they entered the kitchen.

Bundles of tied herbs hung from a rod over the sink, and dozens of jars of canned fruits and vegetables sat on the countertop all in rows.

"My aunt likes to store most of her food for the winter," said Hanna, admiring the display.
"That's neat. My grandma does the same thing," said Notti.

"Have a seat," offered Aunt Lizzy. She pointed to the kitchen table and chairs in front of a picture window framing a large, harvested garden. Notti and Hanna sat down to the aroma of hot apple cider.

"It is apple season Notti, and last weekend Hanna and I went to the apple festival. We bought cider and a bushel of apples to make apple sauce."

"Oh, a bushel sounds like a lot of apples," said Notti, still looking around and taking in all the peculiarities. Aunt Lizzy brought them each a cup of hot cider with a cinnamon stick and then sat in between them. Notti took a sip and relished the flavors flowing over her tongue.

"Hmm, this is really good," said Notti, while Aunt Lizzy took a long look at her.

"Now tell me Notti, what sorts of strangeness have you encountered since arriving here to our little village on the hill?"

"Well," said Notti hesitantly, not knowing where to begin.
"It's okay Notti; you can tell Aunt Lizzy anything. She has all kinds of strange things happen to her too. Isn't, that right?"

"Well, that's partially correct Hanna, but things only seem strange when there's confusion or a misunderstanding as to why they are occurring. There generally is a reason, and it's up to you and to anyone you entrust with these experiences to help you understand them. Now take your time and start from the beginning Notti."

Notti set down her cup, took a deep breath. She began by telling Aunt Lizzy about the first time she saw the water tower and how she almost flew over the neighborhood. She described the pirate dream with Grandpa Pine. And then meeting Patrick on the ship, and again later in class. Notti showed her the dreamtime bracelet, talked about the crows on the playground and about the African storyteller during the history lesson and Patricks magazine about ancient lands.

Hanna looked surprised, but Notti continued. She finished by telling Aunt Lizzy about the bright light she saw around Hanna at the pond. And about the golden ray of light that appeared around them both.

Aunt Lizzy looked into Notti's eyes and gently touched her shoulder.

"I think I can give you an idea of what may be happening," she said with confidence.

"This will take much longer than a cup of cider to explain, so let's begin with this. You, my dear Notti are about to learn and most likely encounter a life changing adventure."

"What? Excuse me?" said Notti.
She looked at Hanna who shrugged her shoulders.
"I told you those crows were trying to tell you something," said Hanna.

Aunt Lizzy nodded and then continued.

"You, dear, dear child are being summoned to learn something by your beloved grandfather. He is trying to communicate to you, and how fortunate that your father's job has brought you to this village. This is the highest point in the entire city with a magical tower."

"Magic, what kind of magic?" asked Notti.

"Well, the tower is believed by some to be in an area of high energy, where what you imagine can become real or manifested. The best way I can explain it is that it's a zone with a high vibration of electromagnetism or cosmic ray energy. It's like a huge antenna that picks up radio wave signals."

"Are you serious?" asked Hanna. "How come you never told me this before?"

"You never asked," said Aunt Lizzy.

"Oh," said Hanna lowering her head.

"Oh, darling girl, it's okay. It's my motto to never push this on to anyone. Whenever you're ready to know more, you can always ask. What a wonderful way for you to begin your inquiries. Especially with a new friend who is in the middle of a unique experience of her own. Magic is a word that's used when an event or a circumstance can't be fully explained. Or has yet to be proven. When I say the tower is magical, I mean there are things that happen around the tower that can't always be explained. However, are real enough for some."

"Oh," said Hanna and Notti at the same time. Aunt Lizzy could see the girls were still a bit confused.

"For example, there was a time in the 1600's when philosophers and clerics thought the earth was the center of the universe. And poor Galileo, a very knowledgeable astronomer, proved it wasn't. He was put under house arrest for the rest of his life because of what he believed. It wasn't his fault that he was ahead of his time. And that those in power couldn't understand his explanations. However, if you're ready to listen and to learn why you're experiencing magic. And and you understand the explanation, then it won't seem so strange to you anymore. "

"I get it," said Notti. "You're saying, that because it's new and I've never experienced it before, that it's strange. But once I understand, I won't think I'm crazy."

Aunt Lizzy laughed and nodded. "Yep, I think you've got it. Whatever you're experiencing now, know that it is real to you. And know that it is coming from your grandfather who is in spirit."

"Tell us what spirit is," said Hanna with renewed enthusiasm.

"Spirit is another level of energy, just like light, wind, water, and the sun are energy, we are also energy. It's obvious Notti that you and your grandfather's energies are very closely tied. Your memory of him keeps you connected to him through your dreams. Now the crows can read your energy field, and they were drawn to you because you vibrated a frequency of light they understood."

Notti and Hanna looked at each other and then back at Aunt Lizzy.

"When you were thinking of your grandfather and the dream, and of Patrick bringing you your bracelet gems, you were also emitting a particular color. The crows merely flew at you to acknowledge they could read your energy."

"Wow, that is so cool," said Hanna as she looked at Notti again. "Just think about that; crows can read you."

"Let's do a little research on the crow," said Aunt Lizzy as she reached over for a large blue book on the shelf.

"Let's check what the indigenous definition of the crow is in my animal spirit guidebook," she said while leafing through the pages. Notti leaned in closer and innocently asked.

"Animal spirit guides, what is that?

"Well, simply put, it's the guardian spirit of an animal. It either appears or can be called upon when you need protection, guidance, inspiration, healing, or encouragement. Every animal symbolically, represents their greatest asset or their contribution as a species. When one appears to you, treat it as a message for what you may need at the time

"That's really cool," said Notti as her eyes widened to see Aunt Lizzy beaming with rays of light surrounding her.

"Now according to the spirit guidebook, the crows are asking you to be very watchful over the next few days. Especially for any signs or omens that will teach or guide you. There is an expected big change coming very soon that will take you into some future events that will directly affect you."

There came a sudden stillness in the air, and Notti could feel her heartbeat accelerating with both fear and excitement.

"Why is this happening to me," whispered Notti?

"Because you're gifted in this way. As you grew your grandfather recognized your gift and accepted and nurtured it. Now that gift is growing and changing as you mature and change."

"Oh," said Notti with a blank stare. She took a long sip of cider and stared out the window.
"Are you okay Notti? Hanna reached over to touch her arm.

"Um, yeah, I'm okay. It's just never been explained to me before. I always thought it was coming from me. I didn't think about it coming to me from someone or somewhere else."

"Well Notti, from what you've told me and Hanna, it's coming to and from you. Now Patrick is a part of this experience, and he may well be going through the same process you're going through. He too is just waking up to his gift," continued Aunt Lizzy with obvious enthusiasm. "You are attracting these experiences to you, and what you need to know is why you're experiencing the images and what to do about them. I think those answers are slowly but surely working their way to you. It's important for you to accept what you see and how it is being revealed to you. I'm quite sure that soon you will understand more, okay?"

"Okay," said Notti as tears began to form. Quickly she tried to blink them back, but it was too late. Aunt Lizzy saw them and immediately stood and took Notti into her arms.

"After all you've experienced, you are deserving of a good cry. Go ahead and let it out. I understand," said Lizzy giving her a squeeze.

"Thank you very much. I'm just happy to hear that I'm not crazy like everyone else thinks I am, everyone of course except my grandparents. I'm okay, really," said Notti as she pulled back and wiped the tears from her eyes.

"Well, you better get home, and we'll visit again when we have more time. In the meantime, try not to worry, don't be afraid, and just go with it, because it's my guess this is only the beginning," said Aunt Lizzy with a pat on Notti's shoulders.

"The beginning of what?" asked Notti, looking deeply into Aunt Lizzy's green eyes.

"The beginning of something your grandfather feels you're ready for," said Aunt Lizzy with a wink and a smile.

The girls finished their cider, and Aunt Lizzy walked them to the door and waited while they put on their shoes. She gave Notti another hug and Hanna an even bigger one.

"Thank you for the cider," said Notti as she stepped out and sat on the bottom step to wait for her father. Aunt Lizzy waved goodbye before closing her little red door. "Thanks Hanna. Your aunt's nice." Notti turned around and saw someone coming up the hill, and instead of her father it was Patrick holding a tennis racket.

Chapter Eight

A GLIMMER OF LIGHT

Patrick," called Notti, as if she'd known him all her life.

"Hi," he said waving his tennis racket. Hanna and Notti caught up to him, but suddenly Notti felt awkward about what to say.

Hanna spoke up when she saw Notti's sudden discomfort.

"Who are you going to play tennis with?"

"Oh, I'm waiting for Cody to get here. He stayed after to do an errand for our scout master. What are you doing on the hill?" he asked.

"We went to Hanna's aunt's house," said Notti, thankful Hanna had stepped in.

She wanted to share with Patrick how magical he had become but couldn't think of how to begin.

"Really, I didn't know your aunt lived up here," he said looking at Hanna.

"Yeah, she grew up here and now lives in my grandma's house."

"Your grandma lives there too?" asked Notti.

"No, my Aunt Lizzy moved in to take care of Granny McDonald last year before she died."

"Your grandma was Granny McDonald?" asked Patrick taking a step back.

"Yeah, she was, why?" asked Hanna while taking a step forward.

"Well, wasn't she a witch or something?"

"Where did you hear that?" asked Hanna with clenched fists.

"My brother's best friend Toby said she was. He used to mow her lawn, and one time he forgot his backpack and ran back to get it just before it got dark. When he got up the hill, he saw her with a bunch of people flying around the tower. They were singing weird songs and playing drums. He got so scared he peed in his pants and ran home.”

Notti looked at Hanna’s red face and asked her.

“Is that another reason why it’s called the Witch’s Tower?”

“She wasn’t a witch; she was a psychic who could see into the future. I would have told you, but I didn’t want you to think my family was crazy or weird,” said Hanna relaxing her fists.

“Is your Aunt Lizzy a psychic too?” asked Notti.

“No, I told you she’s a naturalist, but maybe she is. I don’t know, I’ve never asked her that before.”

Notti looked at Patrick and asked him.

“Do you really think Toby saw Hanna’s grandma flying around the tower?”

“I don’t think he would make it up. My brother wanted to see for himself, but Toby was too scared and wouldn’t go back,” replied Patrick.

Hanna and Notti looked at each other at the same time with raised eyebrows. Hanna followed Patrick’s gaze toward the tower, and Notti looked at Patrick and suddenly a glimmer of light shot out of Patrick’s head and surrounded him like a large halo. From behind his shoulders sprouted a small set of wings and on his wrist appeared a silver band. Notti’s heart raced as she tried to act calm.

“I wouldn’t mind flying above the tower,” said Hanna with a chuckle.

“So, why did you shout out my name when I came into class?” asked Patrick, as he turned his gaze towards Notti.

She hesitated, looked at Hanna and then at her feet. She scratched her hair and kicked a few pebbles.

“I thought I had met you somewhere before, and when I saw you, I was trying to figure out where,” said Notti softly while looking at his wings gently unfold.

“Just tell him Notti, tell him about the dream,” said Hanna.

"What dream?" asked Patrick. Notti squinted, pretending that she was trying to remember. She shrugged her shoulders and cocked her head. The winged image suddenly became brighter and more pronounced. Notti batted her eyes to keep from looking as if she were staring.

"Well, we were on a boat," she began, hoping that was enough.

"That's funny because last night I had a dream I was on a sailboat with my dad, and we were deep sea fishing. I haven't had a dream about my dad since I was in first grade."

Notti continued to watch as the light around him shifted into a beautiful turquoise blue. She thought about asking him about his dad, but decided that it would be prying. She knew how annoying it felt to be asked too many questions.

"Oh, well that's nice," said Notti hoping that would be the end of it.

Hanna cleared her throat. "You were both on a pirate's ship and you helped Notti escape from the pirates. When she woke up you swam into her room and gave her the gems for her bracelet," she said pulling up Notti's sleeve.

Notti gasped.

"Hanna, what are you doing?"

"If Patrick and his brother's friend believe my Granny is a witch, then he'll have to believe your story," she said with a huff.

Patrick looked at the bracelet and his eyes glazed over as if he were in a dream state.

"I gave you gems for a bracelet?" He frowned as he tried to figure out what Notti meant.

"You found the bag of them after it fell out of my pocket," said Notti.

"Never mind, I told you it was a dream," she said backing up. Hanna shrugged her shoulders and said nothing as Patrick headed up the hill.

"Sure!   Well, I 'll see you later," said Patrick while still confused.

"Okay," said Notti as she watched Patrick walk to the courts.

She heard Aunt Lizzy's words echo in her ears.

"Just go with it, because this is only the beginning."

Notti sighed, closed her mouth, and went back to sit on Aunt Lizzy's steps and wait.

"What was that all about?" asked Hanna as she sat down next to Notti.

"I can't talk about it. I'm still trying to understand it myself," said Notti.

"Do you think he knows what you're talking about?"

"Maybe," said Notti, wondering if she should tell Hanna about the wings.

"Oh look, there's my dad," said Notti as she stood and grabbed her backpack.

"Well, I live this way," said Hanna pointing to the right.

"Okay, well I live this way," said Notti pointing to the left.

"Okay, well I'll see you on Monday. Let me know if you have any other dreams."

"Sure, I will. Thanks for letting me meet your aunt, I feel much better."

Hanna nodded and they waved goodbye to each other. Notti tried not to think about her awkward moment with Patrick. She couldn't stop thinking about how he could have given her the bag of gems when it was only a dream?

Chapter Nine

GRANDMA'S CALL

Notti sat quietly at the dinner table wondering if tonight would bring another message from Grandpa Pine. She glanced at the clock and sighed, knowing she had only two hours to clean the kitchen and start her homework before bed. The twins were eating like snails. Rusty ate one lima bean at a time, and Randy had made a tepee with his fish sticks and was trying to bite the tips off before they all tumbled down.

"How was school today?" asked Mr. Pine, looking away from the television news to peer at Notti through his black rimmed glasses.

"Fine," said Notti, not wanting to talk about it. She spooned some tartar sauce on her fish sticks, hoping to make them taste better.

"What was fine about it?"
Notti could feel the interrogation coming, the endless questions, and then the lecture.

"I got put next to a boy who eats his boogers."

"You didn't get put Notti, you were seated," said Mr. Pine looking away for a moment to listen to a local news story. "Okay! Well, I was seated next to Jake, and on the other side of me was seated my new friend Hanna," she said rolling her eyes and taking a hesitant bite of the sauce smothered fish stick.

"Don't roll your eyes at your father," said Mrs. Pine, before taking a bite of her sea scallop.

"That's nice," said Mr. Pine as he got up to change the channel to the national news.

"What's your teacher's name?"

"Mr. Johnson. He's really goofy and wears a red bow tie."

I met him," perked up Mrs. Pine. "I thought he was lovely."

Mr. Pine gave Notti a serious look. "There's nothing goofy about a bow tie. Many men wear them. In fact, the bow tie is often associated with lawyers, doctors, and professors."

"Here it comes," thought Notti as she sat back in her seat and forced down her dinner. She could already feel the nausea rising from her stomach.

"During the thirty-year war of the 17th Century, the Croatians or Croats wore them to keep their shirts closed around their neck because they didn't have buttons. King Louis of France was so impressed with how bravely the Croats fought with their uniform and tie, that he named the tie La Cravat in their honor."

The phone rang and Mrs. Pine stood to answer it. She puckered her lips, patted her dyed auburn brown curls. With her most sophisticated voice she answered the phone.

"Hello, this is Mrs. Terence Pine. Who may I ask is calling?"

"Were you asked to write a summer vacation essay?" continued her father.

"Terence," Dr. Sanchez wants to talk to you about your presentation tonight."

Notti sighed, finished her fish sticks and lima beans with a look of disgust. She washed it down with a gulp of milk and excused herself from the table as the nausea continued to rise.

"I'm going to do my homework," she said to her mother, who was busy dipping her jumbo shrimp into the butter, garlic, and lemon juice.

"If I ever have children, I will never feed them fish sticks, or beans that taste like wax or look like that boy's buggers," thought Notti.

"Don't forget you're doing the dishes and watching the boys tonight," her mother concluded. With a stern look and cheeks so full that for a moment Notti thought she resembled a chipmunk.

"I won't," said Notti sprinting up the stairs and leaping over the creaky steps. She heard her father hang up the phone and she sighed, knowing she had escaped his continued lecture.

Notti skipped into her room and grabbed the history book from her backpack. She turned to the last two pages of the reading assignment And just as she predicted, there was the topic on slavery. There were drawings of slaves captured and chained together by their necks. They were all packed inside the ships bound for America on the Middle Passage. Although disturbing, Notti got comfortable and read on.

The house quieted down after a while. Notti could hear her mother putting the twins to bed, while her dad showered and sang the Blues off key. Notti skimmed over the pages and finished the chapter before answering the topic questions. She slammed the book shut and sauntered back down the stairs with a feeling of dread. She was tired of being the family maid who didn't even get paid.

Shifting into high speed, Notti cleared the table and hurried into the kitchen to load the dishwasher, sweep the floor, and wipe down the counters before racing back up the stairs.

Tiptoeing past the twin's room, she slipped into her room and lay down on her bed with Patrick's comic book just as her mother knocked and opened the door.

"Notti, your father, and I are leaving. We will be back around ten. The boys shouldn't wake up, so you can watch some T.V. if you'd like."

"Okay, Mom," said Notti, opening the comic book as the door closed. She settled back on to her pillow and leafed through images of villagers in a tropical rain forest that stood shadowed by an immense volcanic mountain. She read about how the men mined the caves for precious gems. And who also built large fishponds to raise their food. She liked how the villagers could summon the rain by simply asking and then giving thanks.

Notti wondered why Patrick had given her the comic book. She thought of him and what they had talked about. She also wondered why he hadn't dreamt of his father in two years. Putting down the comic book, she decided to watch a little bit of television.

Notti tip-toed back down the hall to the stairs and made her way down by trying to avoid the creaks. Finally, she gave up and threw her leg over the banister and sailed the rest of the way down. Hopping off, Notti skipped into the kitchen with the hope that her mother had left a few of the shrimp in the refrigerator. Her cell phone rang and startled her. She giggled thinking it was probably her mother calling to tell her not to touch the shrimp.

"Hello," said Notti.

"Hello Notti, it's me, Grandma."

"Hi Grandma, I'm glad you called. How are you?"

"I'm fine Notti, how is my favorite girl?"

"I'm okay. Are you coming for a visit soon?"

"Well, I would like that, but I'll have to wait and talk to your father first. Is he there?"

"No, he and Mom went to the university for his talk, and I'm babysitting."

"Well, we can have a little talk then," she said as Notti got comfortable on the kitchen stool.

"Now tell me Notti, how do you like your new home?"

"It's really different from New Haven," she began.

"Really, why is that?"

Notti told her grandmother all about Tangle Town and the mysterious water tower, the school, her teacher Mr. Johnson, and her new friends.

"Well, it sounds like a very nice and interesting place. Tell me Notti, have you had any dreams since you've been there?"

"Oh yes Grandma, I did."

Notti told her grandma about Grandpa Pine and the pirate ship, about Patrick and the bracelet gems. About the crows in the playground, and finally about Aunt Lizzy. There was a long pause and Notti wondered if she had said too much and tired out her grandma.

"Notti thank you for sharing this with me because I've also been dreaming. The morning you left I had a dream about Grandpa, and he appeared to be saying that it's time for you to learn about your dreams."

"What do you mean Grandma?"

"I mean that Aunt Lizzy is right, and I am so thankful that your friend Hanna took you to meet her. Notti, Grandpa is trying to communicate with you."

"He is, how?"

"He's doing it through your dreams, because he believes it's time for you to learn the secrets of the dreamtime."

"What's the dreamtime?"

"Well, the way it was explained to me is that the dreamtime is a way for spirit ancestors to communicate with their living family members. You see, it is possible for a family member to time travel to any place in the world by holding a vivid memory of a particular ancestor. If you continue to have a close connection with that person, you can be guided through your dreams to them wherever they are."

"Wow, how do you know that?"

"I know because Grandpa told me he could go through the dream portal with the guidance of his grandmother. She taught him, and when I daydreamed about Grandpa and he appeared to me, he indicated that it's time for you to learn about the portal."

"You saw Grandpa too?"

"Yes, in the kitchen," said Grandma Pine.

"How does he do that?"

"I don't know Notti, but he can, and he can see things that most people can't. Once, just after the twins were born, he wanted to see their light or aura, and if like you they would be light carriers."

"Light carriers?"

"Yes, when Grandpa was a boy, his grandmother told him a story of how all children are born as vessels of perfect light. She said, that if the child is taught to tend the light and not fill it with stones of fear, jealousy and hate, the child will look upon the world with gratitude, love, and respect, and always be a light carrier. Grandpa spent a lot of time helping you to tend your light. He appreciated your vivid imagination, and how you can see the world differently.

"Oh," said Notti, with gladness that she made Grandpa feel happy.

"I remember once when I saw a green light over Grandpa's head, and he said I was looking at his spirit. And today I saw that Patrick was glowing in a light."

"Oh my, did you tell Patrick?'

"No," frowned Notti, "I knew he'd think I was crazy."

"Yes, I suppose if someone is not familiar with this kind of natural phenomena you would be concerned with what they think. Listen, now that you have the bracelet gems, you will need to put one of the many special gemstones inside a bezel on your bracelet.

Grandpa will find a way to help you choose so you can travel through the dream portal to a specific time and place. Until then, just imagine him in your mind and he will guide you."

"That sounds amazing," said Notti as she felt the excitement pumping through her like an electric charge.

"Have you gone through the dreamtime, Grandma?"

"No, I haven't Notti. My family didn't practice such things. After Grandpa and I were married for a while, he finally felt comfortable enough to share this knowledge with me."

Notti listened while Grandma Pine explained how disappointed they were with Notti's father. That he showed no interest in anything to do with the natural or spirit world. Grandpa Pine returned the bracelet to his mother for safekeeping. He believed that no one in the family would ever learn this ancient belief and tradition.

Grandma Pine told Notti how the dreamtime went back to ancient times, where the practice taught dreamers that all time, past, present, and future occurred at the same time. Notti sat in awe listening to her grandmother share what she knew about Grandpa's secret.

"I'm sorry we can't be together Notti. I wish I could have shared this with you before you left. I'm glad we have this time now."

Notti heard a car door slam and quickly looked at the clock. They had talked for over an hour, and it was late.

"Grandma, Mom, and Dad are back. Do you want to talk to them?"

"No, I'll phone them tomorrow. It's late and we should both get to sleep. You are welcome to share this with your parents if you feel comfortable. So, I'll say good night and send you my love for success in your dreamtime education and adventures."

"Good night, Grandma, and thank you for calling."

Notti hung up just as her parents walked in through the back door.

"Notti, you're still up?" asked her mother.

"Yeah, I've been talking to Grandma. She said she'll call you tomorrow."

"Oh, well we ran a little longer because you father had to meet the staff members of his department."

"How did it go Dad?"

"It went well, and I think most people found my talk on romance languages to be stimulating and interesting."

"That's nice," said Notti.

"How's Grandmother?" asked Mrs. Pine, while removing her coat and hat.

"Fine, she just wanted to know how I liked my new home and school."

Notti headed up the stairs while thinking about what they had really talked about. She heard the liquor cabinet door open, and knew her parents would settle into the living room for what her father called their night cap. She tip-toed past the boy's room and quietly stepped into her room. Near her bed she looked down on the floor to see the Mu Land comic book. It sat opened to a page with a woman holding a gemstone between two fingers.

"Hmm," said Notti as she retrieved her gem bag and took out the red ruby gem and set it on her nightstand.

"I wonder how this gem works"?

The full moon turned the bedroom into a glowing wonderland. Light reflected off the mirror and walls and bounced over the furniture.

Notti put on her nightgown and slipped under the covers. She fiddled with her bracelet, yawned, and thought of her grandpa. She rolled over on to her side and fell asleep and soon into her dreamtime adventure.

Notti suddenly found herself outside on a pile of dried fallen leaves. Somewhere in the distance she could hear the faint sound of a beating drum.

Chapter Ten

THE RUBY GEM

"Notti are you coming?" whispered Patrick. Notti stirred and yawned and opened her eyes to find Patrick standing over her with a flashlight.

"We should have told you to bring a flashlight, but you can use mine."

"What are you talking about?" asked Notti while listening to the steady drumbeat.

"Don't you want to go up to the tower and meet Hanna? The good witches are here for a ritual or a ceremony."

"What good witches?"

"The ones from the neighborhood," he said pointing to the water tower.

"Why are they there?"

"Because it's the full moon," said Patrick while handing her his flashlight. Notti jumped up and brushed off the leaves. Hanna came running down the hill with excitement in her eyes.

"I went up near the tower and I saw the drummers. Come on, we can get a good look at the witches if we go up through the woods."

"Witches, I thought you said they were psychics," whispered Notti.

"I didn't say they were psychics; I said my grandma was. Anyway, I think these witches are gonna' dance or do something weird," said Hanna.

Notti felt confused and looked at Patrick who was nodding in agreement.

They took off, and Notti followed close behind. Up and around the pond they jogged. On to the path they continued until they reached the top. Hanna led them to a large boulder, where they turned off their flashlights and crouched down.

"What if they catch us spying on them?" whispered Notti.

"They'll cast a spell on us and turn us into witches too," said Hanna.

Notti's eyes bugged out like a toad, and she blinked back her fear. Inching her way up from behind the boulder, she quickly peeked. Near a patch of woods sat three men dressed in brown tunics beating drums with large sticks.

"I don't see any witches, just three men who look like monks," said Notti sitting back down. Hanna and Patrick took a quick look, and Patrick grabbed Notti's arm.

"Look, they're coming," he whispered.

Notti crept back up to see people stepping out one by one from around the tower. They watched an Asian woman in a kimono with long ballerina arms fluttering delicately like butterfly wings. She bowed to acknowledge the drummers and then stepped aside. A Native American man fully dressed in buckskin leather and a beaded headdress bowed next. Then he stepped aside and a half-veiled woman in a beautifully decorated burka stepped up next and bowed. One by one each uniquely dressed person in traditional garb bowed. They each stepped aside into a circle around the tower. The drums continued to pound out a rhythmic song. Notti's foot gently tapped to the inviting beat. As the last person joined the circle, they all raised their arms together. Then gazed attentively at the brilliant full moon.

"They still don't look like witches to me," whispered Notti.

Hanna and Patrick watched as all the people began to chant a beautiful song. The chant vibrated through Notti and rose within her. It touched her heart with joy and peace. She loved it and wondered what it meant. The drummers suddenly hit their drums harder. They cried out just as a flash of white lightning hit the roof of the tower. Notti and her friends gasped and fell back on their heels. The light spread and engulfed the chanters, changing each into an enormous owl.

The owls took flight and soared toward the top of the tower. They circled again and again, higher, and higher, faster, and faster. Creating a whisking sound with their large wingspan. The speed of the circling owls created a large, blurred ring. It gradually expanded flat like the rings of Jupiter. The rings turned a bright cobalt blue and then dropped. It burst into droplets of darting glowing lights shooting in every direction. From the glow floated out the same men and women. But this time they were dressed in black gowns in hooded red capes. Notti, Hanna, and Patrick couldn't believe their eyes as they watched in amazement.

The capped people continued to chant, only louder. One of the drummers picked up the flute. He played a variation of sweet sounds around their haunting voices. Suddenly, Notti felt herself rising above the ground without any effort. She became frightened and her heart pounded. She couldn't make herself stop. She could see Patrick floating up beside her, and Hanna in a panic, reached for them and called their names. Patrick looked stunned and Notti wanted to scream, but Aunt Lizzy's words echoed in her ears. "Don't be afraid, just go with it."

They floated towards the chanters and then abruptly stopped a couple of yards in front of a woman. She floated toward them, lifted off her hood, removed her veil and smiled.

"Aunt Lizzy, is that you?"

She nodded and rom her pocket she pulled out three ruby gemstones. She placed one in Notti's hand and one on Patrick's. Aunt Lizzy said nothing but floated back into the glowing circle. Notti looked down at Hanna still standing behind the boulder with her hands over her mouth.

"What about Hanna; why doesn't she get the other one?"

Aunt Lizzy followed Notti's gaze and floated to Hanna who was now shaking her head in disbelief. Aunt Lizzy reached for her hands and gently pulled her up. Hanna stared at her aunt before finally speaking.

"Aunt Lizzy, what's happening?"

"Do you want this experience, and if so, are you ready?"

"I don't know," she said looking over at Notti holding the gem.

"Just say the word, yes or no, and if it's yes, then Grandma McDonald will be your guide. She has your bracelet and is waiting for you Hanna, and so is Patrick's grandmother also waiting. Aunt Lizzy held it over Hanna's hand. Hanna looked at the gem and then at Aunt Lizzy.

"Okay, I'm ready," said Hanna in an excited whisper.

"Good. There's nothing to fear. You have
your grandma, you have me, and you have your
friends," she said placing the gem in Hanna's
hand.

"Put it somewhere safe until you have your
bracelet from great Grandma McDonald. And
Notti, Patrick and Hanna, please understand that
the ruby gem will help you to have courage and
ward off negative energies.

Notti sighed when she saw Hanna holding the gem. Looking
at her own gem brought on her tears. She wept at the beauty of
Hanna and her aunt accepting each other. The tears became
blinding, so she closed her eyes to fully enjoy the moment. Quite
suddenly she was moving swiftly but gently and still clutching
her gem. She tried to open her eyes, but she couldn't. She
smelled roses and evergreens, the ocean, and the salt air, and she
wondered why. She felt the warmth of the sun, the cool breeze of
the trade winds, and the flute melody filled her with joy.

Her pounding heart slowed, and her breath became calm. She
sensed something soft yet firm on the back of her neck. Also,
something warm draped over her chest. She thought of Patrick
and Hanna and wondered if they were experiencing everything
she was. Finally, she opened her eyes, only to find that she was
under the covers and back in her bed.

"Oh, I had another dream," she whispered, feeling a slight
twinge in the palm of her hand.   She opened her hand to see the
ruby gem glimmer in the moonlight. Although small, she held it
close to the bracelet to see if it was the right size. Carefully
holding the gem over one of the empty bezels, she placed it in.
Instantly it sealed tight. The bracelet vibrated gently, and Notti
felt delighted at how beautifully the bracelet glistened on her
wrist. She glanced around her room expecting someone or
something to appear, but nothing happened.

"Hmm," she said curiously, remembering all she had seen and
heard.

"All those things made me calm, and then somehow I came out
of my dream," she thought. Looking at her bracelet again she
relaxed her head on the pillow, she closed her eyes and thought
again of Grandpa Pine. She remembered him tucking her in after
a bedtime story with a generous smile and plenty of kisses on her

cheeks, forehead, and nose. Good night my darling Notti, and sweet dreams, he would always whisper. He would turn off the light and the room would turn pitch black, but she never felt alone as she listened to the crickets and to the smell of his cigar from the kitchen. Notti was soon asleep, and with the sound of her first little snore, the gem glimmered, and the bracelet gently hummed.

Chapter Eleven

THE PAINTED MEN

Notti awoke and blinked rapidly at the sunlight pouring warmth upon her face. She stretched the kinks from her arms and legs before noticing that something felt very different.

Slowly, as if being cooked by the sun, her bedroom began to melt away and disappear into an unfamiliar landscape. With a sense of urgency, Notti jumped from her bed in time to watch the dresser and the remains of the bedroom evaporate into a grassy field, where one lone tree stood and resembled an enormous, opened umbrella.

"Oh no," she said panicked. "This is another dreamtime."

She saw nothing but tall grass everywhere for miles and miles in three directions, and in the distance, something moving caught her eye. She could clearly see a person running towards her holding something long. Within seconds, a bald and dark man with white circles painted on his face, leaped in front of her. He danced around wildly with his spear. Notti clutched her chest and screamed as the man made jabbing motions all around her with his spear. He let out a pulsating screech and ran off down a path. Into the brush he leaped with his waist cloth wrap flapping and a cloud of dust trailing his hurried feet.

Notti took a step back and slowly turned around again and again. The air felt exhaustingly hot and humid, and behind her stood a dense forest. She dropped to her knees and cried out.

"What's happening to me? This must be a bad dream."

She screamed, "wake up Notti, wake up!" She pinched herself, squeezed her eyes open and shut, but nothing changed. The piercing sound of a low whistle whizzed past her head and landed an arm's length away with a thud. A large vibrating spear lodged in the ground sent her heart racing. It amplified throughout her body until she felt paralyzed. Another low whistle and another thud ended her frozen stance, just as another spear landed behind her foot.

She jumped up and looked over her shoulder in time to see a mob of feathered men running through the field towards her. Notti screamed and forced her legs to run through the dense tall grass. All the while expecting another whistle and another thud. She ran with a speed fueled by fear and survival. She could hear the yelps and howls quickly gaining upon her. Another spear whistled past her ear. She hoped she'd make it to the forest where she could hide. Over and through the brush she leaped, holding up the hem of her nightgown. Not daring to look back at her pursuers.

"I'm going to die with a spear through my back," she cried out almost out of breath. The ground suddenly shook with a thunderous roar. An earthquake was her first fear as she imagined the land splitting open and swallowing her up.

Instead, a surge of men exploded from the forest with spears and shields and led by the man with the painted circles. Notti had just enough time to leap out of the way and dive behind a pile of rocks as they stampeded by.

Screams and the clashing of spears bombarded her ears. Cautiously she peered up to see a fierce battle underway. There was no hesitation, just jabbing and spearing of flesh and shields. Notti shuddered at the sight and wondered for a moment if she should run, but to where? Without any sense of direction to guide her she remained stuck and in shock.

The painted men soon outnumbered the retreating feathered men. With a victorious and renewed vitality, they chased the feathered men all back to wherever they had come from.

Visibly shaken, Notti crept up from behind the rocks and grabbed on to a larger rock to steady herself. She glanced at her bracelet, and the red gem flashed and radiated like an alarm. A low murmur resonated from the returning warriors. Notti crouched back down and curled up into a small ball. She was hoping to camouflage herself amongst the large rocks.

"They're coming back," she thought as the murmur grew louder. Abruptly, the voices stopped. Within the dead silence came only the sound of the breeze as Notti trembled uncontrollably.

A bloodied hand grabbed Notti's shoulder and pulled her up. Startled, she leaped to her feet and landed within a circle of glaring men. All holding their blood-stained weapons. They stood poised and ready to attack. Although Notti continued to shake, she somehow managed to blurt out.

"Please don't kill me. I don't know where I am."

The silence and glares intensified. Notti burst into tears sobbing. The red gem continued to glow like a beacon from a lighthouse giving her courage. The leader smiled and waved his hand, beckoning Notti to follow them.

Chapter Twelve

SERPENT URAEUS

Minutes passed and still the warriors held their positions. With curious stares and nostrils flaring like a raging bull. Notti wiped away her tears and sighed. She figured she would have been dead by now if they were going to kill her. She noticed how they weren't much taller than herself. They were built with long torsos and short muscular legs. Their wraps were tucked up between their legs like a flat diaper. Around their necks hung a diamond shaped wooden pendant. Their hair was either braided, shaven, or curly. Notti knew she was staring. She marveled at how different they were from anyone she had ever seen before.

Other warriors soon returned from the chase, including the lead warrior with his painted white circles. He pushed his way through the crowd. He turned to three other men and spoke quietly amongst them. When he finished, all eyes turned back to Notti.

The warriors all rested the ends of their spears to the ground. Notti finally stopped shaking. The leader took several small steps towards Notti and gently reached for her hand. He held it up to show everyone her beaming silver bracelet. Notti's heart skipped a beat as she stood rooted to and not daring to move. A chorus of cheers ended the silence, and the leader dropped her hand and motioned to a warrior with painted stripes on his face.

The striped warrior maneuvered his way through the crowd to stand next to Notti. The gem on her bracelet stopped glowing and Notti felt his piercing eyes upon her. She hoped he wouldn't take her bracelet. To her surprise he motioned to Notti to follow him as everyone formed a straight line. Slowly the warriors began their walk back into the forest. They passed the feathered dead laying scattered in the grass. Notti shuddered when they pulled the spears from their limp bodies. They lifted their own dead and wounded and carried them in a cloth like hammock over their shoulders. Notti couldn't help but wonder what the battle was about.

Notti moved along a dusty path through the brush and around sun baked boulders. She could feel the dry grass under her feet crunch and crumble with every step. She hadn't realized how moist she'd become. Sweat now ran down her back like a mini waterfall. She noticed the backs of the men were shinny and wet.

And wishfully thought of how much a gust of wind would help relieve them all.

Soon they stopped at the banks of a narrow river. Holding their spears high above their heads, they plunged in and began to cross over.

"Please don't let there be a snake or a crocodile hiding under the rocks or behind any floating logs," whispered Notti. Her arms quickly sprouted goose bumps. Taking small steps, she lifted her night gown. She tried to balance herself against the current by gripping the rocks with her toes. The water felt refreshing. She was reminded of her swim with Patrick off the pirate ship.

A deep sounding shrill ran through the line of men, and Notti strained to look between them for the cause. She gasped when she saw at least ten water snakes swimming across the surface. They looked larger than any snake she had ever seen. They glided with ease to form two strategic lines on either side of them. Horrified, she quickly hid behind her guide to watch. Three warriors waded towards the reptiles. They hummed a low resonating sound and held their diamond shaped pendants up to their foreheads. Several other warriors stood poised and ready with their spears.

"I'm really going to die now. I'm going to be swept away by the current. Then bitten by a snake. I'll drown before I ever find out where I am or why I'm here," said Notti to her guide. He paid no attention, but continued his intense look at the snakes.

Notti's red gem glowed again, and without warning everything in the air changed. The sky grew dark, clouds suddenly formed, and heavy gusts of wind whirled around them.

From a large rain cloud came a streak of lightning. It hit next to the snakes, and they quickly dispersed in all directions. Panic struck as everyone tried to stumble across. The rain clouds engulfed the sun and sent buckets of rain down to drench the party. Notti was instantly soaked, and her night gown clung to her like saran wrap.

The rain stopped just as quickly as it had come. Another bolt of lightning charged across the darkened sky, followed by a boom of thunder. The drama sent a shiver through Notti. The guide grabbed her hand just as another bolt of lightning struck, hitting a large tree near the shore. The tree burst into flames and crashed over the now crazed snakes. From the flames surged a plume of smoke. From the smoke emerged a giant green serpent ten times the size of the water snakes.

Notti's head tilted back as she stared in awe at the monstrous rising reptile. There was something serene about the serpent. The warriors must have seen it too because they stopped scrambling over one another. The serpent's eyes gently gazed down upon them, and together the warriors all bowed their heads in reverence. Everyone huddled together as the rain clouds moved on, taking the drama with them. A ray of sunlight appeared and surrounded the serpent like a warm blanket. It hissed and darted its tongue again and again. The water snakes stopped their crazed swimming and curiously raised their heads.

A mist dispersed the light and settled around the serpent. The painted man gestured for everyone to finish crossing over. Notti followed taking careful but hurried steps past the hypnotized snakes. The misted serpent rose majestically from the water to the very tip of its tail. It flickered its tongue several times before it began to spin. It spun slowly at first, and then faster and faster with the force of a tornado, turning the river into a whirlpool. Snakes were instantly forced into the center, and though they scrambled to break free, the force sucked them down into its drain one by one, until they all disappeared.

The serpent slowed the spinning until the river calmed and then slowly it lowered itself into the river until it disappeared.

Notti stood in awe as warriors hurried to attend to the dead and wounded again. Questions raced through Notti's head as she asked herself how, what, and where such a creature could have come from.

When everyone had gathered and formed another line, the bald painted man waved his arm, and they continued their trek down a narrow path into the great green forest. Notti stumbled along as the shock continued to hold on.

"Don't be afraid," she whispered. She followed her guide into the lush foliage with creeping vines and colorful flowers everywhere. High pitched screeches and muffled noises echoed around them, as they picked up the pace down the winding dirt path.

Notti wondered if the noises were birds or wild animals. She took in small glimpses of the sky when it appeared between the treetops. She took careful steps to ensure her footing and watched for anything crawling or slithering by. Her memory of the snakes left her heart still pounding and her stomach tied in a knot.

She tripped over a tree root and fell against the striped man with such a force, that he stumbled and fell against the man in front of him. One by one the men toppled like a row of dominos. Within seconds the whole line of men had fallen on top of each other in one long heap.

Notti didn't know why, but she couldn't move. She closed her eyes and lay there listening to the commotion. Finally, she opened her eyes to see the striped man standing over her with a leather bag. He placed the spout to her lips, and she opened her mouth to cool water running down her dry throat. She wanted to thank him. But before she could speak, she was lifted by two men and placed on a large cloth like hammock. They carried her through the forest as she lay still. Shewatched sparks of sunshine and the blue-sky peek through layers upon layers of tropical branches and leaves. The gentle rocking calmed her nerves and her thoughts. Gradually the rhythm of the trek put her to sleep, and once again she dreamt of Grandpa Pine.

In his metal boat sat Grandpa Pine rowing down the middle of the river. Notti sat cross-legged on a dock watching him talk, but she couldn't understand a single word. Grandpa Pine pointed to his wrist and then to her bracelet, and when she looked at the gem it glowed brightly. Grandpa smiled, and with great ease he turned his boat around and disappeared around the bend.

Chapter Thirteen

A VILLAGE OF CLAY

Notti awoke into darkness and quiet. She searched her mind for an explanation but could see only a small opening in a wall. Rolling on to her knees, she stood up and bumped her head on a very low ceiling

"Ouch!" she yelled, rubbing her head, and crouching back down on to her knees. Crawling to the opening, she stuck her head out and looked around.

"Oh my," she said looking at the many clay huts with straw roofs, and with children chasing each other around them. Mothers with babies wrapped to their backs stood mashing something in a deep wooden bowl with a wide stick. A small circle of men sat crossed legged carving wooden spears, talking, and laughing, and young boys herded goats into a nearby field.

Scooting back inside, Notti sat down to think through her dilemma.

"Am I a prisoner or a guest?"

There were no bars on the windows and no one standing guard. She heard footsteps outside, and a shadow appeared in the opening. Notti could feel her heart flutter as she watched and waited. A young girl popped her head inside and smiled at Notti, who in return smiled back. The girl set down a bowl of food and another bowl of something to drink. She motioned to Notti to eat, before crawling in and sitting down beside her.

Notti inched herself up to the bowl and immediately the delicious aroma reached her nostrils. With neither a fork nor a spoon, Notti scooped up a small fingerful to taste a sweet potato. With another fingerful she ate white meat and yellow rice. The hunger surged through her, and Notti stuffed herself, taking sheer delight in all the flavors.

Finishing with a gulp of tasty, sweet juice, she licked her fingers and rubbed her full round belly. Notti thanked the girl with a nod and a smile. The girl nodded and smiled back but couldn't help but look at Notti's dirty and torn nightgown.

Another shadow appeared at the opening, and a woman came in with a basin of water and a bundle of cloths. She whispered something to the girl, who picked up the empty bowls and left. The light poured in through the opening and cast a silhouette of the woman.

Notti felt her gentle gaze, and when the woman placed a hand over her own heart, she very slowly said, "War-a." Notti leaned closer and repeated her name, "Wara."

Wara smiled and pointed to Notti. Notti placed her hand over her own heart and very slowly said, "Not-ti." Wara nodded and clearly said, "Notti."

Wara scooted up to Notti holding the large basin of water and a rag. She pointed to it and then tugged at her own dress. Notti understood, and carefully Wara began to undress her and bathe her from head to toe. She rinsed Notti's face and wiped and washed away the dried mud and leaves from her legs and feet. She dressed Notti in a colorful wrap which she tied around her chest. She untangled her hair with a wooden comb that looked like a large fork. When Wara finished, she gathered everything into a small bundle and set it outside the opening.

Carefully, she crouched through the opening and gestured for Notti to follow. Notti went through the opening awkwardly in her cloth wrap. In the sunlight she was able to clearly see the woman who called herself Wara.

Notti thought she looked beautiful. Her dark skin glistened in the sun like Grandma's brewed coffee. Her eyes shined brightly, and her full cheeks reminded Notti of her mother. A penny-sized mole lay above her left eyebrow just like her dad's, and she stood a little taller than Notti.

"I like her, and I think she likes me too," thought Notti.

They walked together hand in hand through the village, with Wara occasionally stopping to chat with her neighbors. Notti could hear her own name in a long procession of sounds, so she knew they were talking about her.

She watched the women push their babies up higher on to their backs. The toddlers gathered in a small cluster around their mother's legs. They stared at Notti, the foreign visitor with their wide and curious eyes but spoke not a word.

Notti noticed how happy they appeared to be without diapers. At her home, babies never walked nor crawled around naked. She remembered watching the babies at the beach, waddling around like ducklings with soggy diapers hanging between their legs.

"They would probably love it here," she whispered with a smile.

A few of the toddlers smiled back, and Notti felt a glow of acceptance come over her. She wanted to bend down and scoop them up into her arms for a hug. However, Wara appeared to be saying her goodbyes, so Notti just gave them each a bigger smile.

A cheerful woman handed Wara a large leather water bag on a strap, which she took and flung it over her shoulder. The woman also handed her a large bundle with bedding and a basket of food, which Wara balanced on her head. Then like the baldheaded man, the woman gently took Notti's hand with the bracelet and held it up to her eyes to examine. She nodded to Wara as she let go of Notti's hand.

"They know something about this bracelet," thought Notti as she and Wara walked out of the village. Soon they were greeted by a cluster of older children who huddled together whispering and pointing at Notti. A tall man with a fat bundle on his head and holding a walking stick strolled by. The children crowded around him as he handed out pieces of what looked like beef jerky. They all laughed gleefully, biting off pieces, chewing, and skipping around one another.

Notti remembered when Grandpa Pine came back from the store, pretending he hadn't bought anything for her. She laughed to herself thinking about how she would dance around him like a bumble bee. She would ask him over and over again what he had bought. Finally, he would pull from his pocket her favorite treat, a bag of black licorice. They'd walk down the driveway, biting off pieces, chewing, and laughing as they talked about their day.

"Grandpa," she whispered, watching the old man as she and Wara left the camp with the echo of children's laughter behind them.

Chapter Fourteen

THE LONG PATH

Wara and Notti followed a path through the tall wheat-colored grass. To their left stood proud and noble mountains displaying rugged profiles. To their right breathed the dense jungle from where Notti had arrived from. Behind them the village grew further and further away, until it disappeared into the warm golden landscape of the plains.

Notti hadn't thought much about where they might be going or why, but she had a feeling it wasn't close. The empty land stretched for miles, and she felt a little nervous, especially having witnessed her first battle. She knew Grandpa Pine was watching over her. So, she mustered up her courage and followed Wara, her new friend who would hopefully lead her somewhere safe.

Wara took long and graceful steps while balancing the large bundle perfectly on her head. Notti had to sprint just to catch up, but soon she grew comfortable in her new wrap. She fell into step with Wara, while swinging her arms back and forth. From a distance the two glided along like roller skaters in complete harmony against a crisp blue sky. The grass whistled when the wind blew across it like a lonely bird singing the Blues. Notti looked down at her bracelet just as the gem began to glow. Her heart skipped a beat as she searched the fields for any signs of danger. Although she saw nothing unusual, what she heard nearly stopped her in her tracks.

"Welcome, welcome," whispered a man's voice. Notti looked around, but saw no one, and Wara appeared to be focused on the path. Notti knew that she didn't speak her language, so who could be whispering, she wondered? A rush of excitement and anticipation shot through her as the voice continued.

"We have been waiting for your arrival.
Learn well so you understand what will come."

Feeling more bewildered and puzzled, Notti searched again, for the voice sounded as clear as the day. Wara turned to look at Notti and gestured for her to catch up. Notti wondered if she also heard the whisper. Suddenly she felt much like she' felt when Grandpa Pine told a ghost story. She listened and looked boldly from side to side, but there was nothing. Shaking her head and shrugging it off, as she decided it must be her imagination.

With the sun rising higher in the east, Notti knew they were heading south. She looked to the west, and she saw a figure moving through the grass. Wara neither slowed nor stopped. Soon a tall and slender woman stepped onto their path in front of Wara, carrying a bundle on her head and a water bag over her shoulder. She joined them but walked in silence, wearing a similar colorful wrap. Her taller height led Notti to think that perhaps she was of a different tribe. Notti looked back and saw neither a village nor any huts, but only mountains and trees. She couldn't help but wonder why the woman had joined them on the path, or where they were going.

The path led them out of the grassland through a large grove of trees with long swaying branches that resembled the strumming fingers of a guitarist. Notti thought she heard someone singing, but when she looked around, there was no one. A swift wind rustled the branches as they entered the grove. Her heart skipped another beat when she suddenly heard someone singing.

"Young one, we meet you at last.
Pay close attention to the signs you pass.
And to the dreams that unfold,
revealing stories yet untold.
Watch and listen young one,
And you will learn."

Notti scanned the treetops and searched through the branches, but still there was no one. As she lowered her gaze back to the path, her eyes met Wara's smiling eyes, and she nodded. Notti again wondered if Wara heard the song, but she had already turned away without missing a step. Notti shook away her thoughts and decided that what she heard was real even if Wara and the other woman didn't hear the song. Taking a deep breath of acceptance, Notti returned to watching the path as they continued on.

Soon they were led to a wide sloping valley, and the two women adjusted their bundles a little further back on their heads. Notti tightened and adjusted her wrap, which was beginning to slip down. Once secured, she looked up just as another figure in the distance came towards them. Notti squinted hoping to see better, but not until the figure stepped onto the path did, she realize it was again another woman.

On her head the woman also balanced a bundle, and she elegantly placed herself in front of everyone. No one said a word, but kept up the same pace, even as the path continued into the valley. Confused, Notti gritted her teeth to keep from bursting out with questions that couldn't be answered.

She figured they had been walking for most of the day, stopping only to take a drink of water, eat a few pieces of jerky, and relieve themselves behind a bush. The sun had already peaked and was slowly making its way down, and still they continued across the largest valley Notti had ever seen.

Surprisingly, they saw no animals along the way. Notti briefly thought about the serpents and decided to be grateful that nothing had crossed their path. She felt a shift in her sense of direction when she realized that somewhere along the way they had turned without her notice. The mountains were now directly in front of them.

"I hope we get to wherever we're going soon, or we're going to be walking in the dark," she whispered while looking up to the sky.

A sudden high-pitched moan startled Notti, and a man's voice that knew her name spoke up.

"Notti, walk on to me and follow the path, to find the answers you seek."
Notti shivered when she heard the voice call her name. She worried someone might be hiding behind the massive piles of rock along the mountain path. When she walked past and looked, there was no one. A gust of wind fluttered her long wrap and tangled around her legs forcing her to stop. Wara instinctively stopped and ran back, and so did the other two women. Wara gently touched Notti's shoulder. Notti looked up and watched

her take one hand to steady the bundle on her head, and with her other hand to straighten Notti's wrap.

Tears welled up in Notti's eyes, and the bracelet began to glow. She cried for the confusion, for fear of the unknown, and for being so far away from home. Wara pulled Notti close to her with a loving embrace, as Notti let the tears flow down her cheeks.

Relaxing into Wara's nurturing arms, Notti sighed when she gave her a squeeze then let go. Wara nodded to the other women, who picked up their bundles to trek up a winding path.

Notti wiped her eyes and followed close behind. They walked until the light of day dimmed. Notti looked to the horizon to watch the sunset and turn the sky into a beautiful display of red, pink, and orange. Soon the darkness would settle in. Picking up their pace, they climbed steadily around boulders and shrubs under the light of a crescent moon.

"I hope we're not going to walk all night," thought Notti as the air cooled, and the path zigzagged on its way up. Notti breathed a little harder in the thinner air. Weary, she dragged herself up the mountain side, then turned another corner. To her surprise they stepped into a campground with a small fire pit and a grass hut.

Notti sighed with relief as everyone set down their bundles and began gathering firewood. The two women stacked the sticks and branches into the pit and Wara disappeared behind the hut into the coming night. The women continued preparing the pit just as a spark flashed from behind the hut. Notti watched as a small but bright light swayed from side to side towards her. She nervously stood her ground, and was just about to shout out a warning, when the light exposed Wara holding a black pot with burning coals that she dropped into the pit. Within seconds there was a blazing fire.

"Hmm," said Notti as she pondered how a pot of coals could be waiting for them on a mountain side.

"Maybe they were close to another camp," she thought as she quickly stood close to the fire and watched her goose bumps disappear. One woman unpacked her bundle while the other tended to the fire. Wara pulled from her bag something wrapped in large green leaves. She set it alongside the coals and waved to Notti to follow her.

Wara took her inside the hut and pointed to a large woven mat and made a sitting motion. Notti sat down. From a pile in the corner, Wara pulled out two goat skins sewn together. She laid the skins over Notti to rest.

Notti yawned and tried to get comfortable, but she could smell something cooking on the fire. Although she couldn't tell what it was, her thoughts drifted off. She thought once again about her predicament.

"This is a strange dreamtime. Why am I here, and what am I supposed to do?"

Notti could hear steam or something sizzling, and the women were talking in hushed voices. Wara stepped back in with a small clay bowl and a cup. She handed them to Notti and sat down beside her on the edge of the mat.

"Thank you," said Notti as she bit into a root vegetable. Wara hummed herself, and Notti took a bite of fish. She was a little hungry since her last meal, and the food tasted delicious.

Wara's song felt soothing, and she stayed until Notti finished her meal. Wara began to make her way out, and Notti cleared her throat to gently speak to her.

"Thank you, Wara. I feel much better now."

Wara nodded as if she understood.

"I wish we could talk to each other so I could tell you about myself," continued Notti while trying to hold back a yawn.

"I'm not sure where I am or why I'm here, but thank you for taking care of me," concluded Notti with another yawn.

Slipping down under the goat skin, Notti was asleep within minutes. Wara quietly backed out of the hut with an affectionate look at her young traveler on the side of a mountain.

Chapter Fifteen

THE FLOATING LADY

A loud crack followed by a boom woke Notti with a jolt from her slumber. The thunder boomed so loudly that she was sure it hovered right over their little hut. Wara popped her head in and gently tickled Notti's feet. Notti giggled and wondered if she really had to get up, or could she pretend it was Sunday morning and just sleep in. Another boom followed by a louder crack of lightening, sat her straight up. Wara helped her to stand, then rolled up the goat skin and tucked it under her arm. The two stepped into the cool morning mountain air, and Notti could see the storm moving in with its massive dark clouds. She looked down at the smoldering campfire and realized there would be no breakfast.

The women were lifting their bundles back on to their heads and were ready to leave. Wara gently touched Notti on the shoulder and motioned for her to follow. Notti adjusted her wrap since it had loosened during the night. She trekked past the campground and suddenly stopped and tightened her legs and bottom.

"I have to go," she shouted holding herself.

Wara turned and nodded that she understood. Notti ran and found a large bush to hide behind and managed to pull her wrap up and squat.

"It's times like this I wish I were a boy," she thought with a sigh of relief.

A rainbow spanned the sky just as Notti stepped out from behind the bush. A flock of strange black birds landed on a dead tree branch above, and she thought about the crows on the playground and wondered what day it was.

"Hmm!" she said, returning to the path only to find that Wara and the women were gone.

"Wara, where are you?"

Notti ran up the path calling her name. "Wara, Wara, wait for me."

The storm exploded, causing her to stumble over clumps of grass and scattered rocks. She teetered forward but kept herself from falling. She ran breathless around another curve hidden by larger boulders. The hill became so steep that Notti had to lift her wrap to keep from tripping. She was just about to call Wara's name again when she rounded another corner and stopped. Notti stood frozen at the entrance to a large encampment overlooking another deep valley.

Several yards away sat Wara on a long rock platform surrounded by a small crowd of men and women. Everyone was dressed colorfully in tunics and elaborate headdresses of small gold stones and black and white feathers. Seated in front of the platform were several boys and girls who looked around her own age.

A woman sitting next to Wara, brought her fist down on a large drum. The boys and girls raised their right hands just as the sun peeked out briefly from behind the oncoming rain clouds. Its rays covered the children, and on every wrist, there glimmered a gemmed silver bracelet. Notti stood in awe, as two women rushed over and led her across the campground to sit next to the other children. Notti could feel all eyes on her as she sat down near the end of the row. A girl sitting next to a boy smiled at Notti, showing her dimples and deep brown eyes. Notti smiled back and watched as the girl touched the boy's shoulder and the stones in his bracelet glowed.

The next boy touched the shoulder of the boy next to him, who then touched the shoulder of a girl seated next to him. Her gem lit up, and she then touched the shoulder of the girl next to her. All down the line the children touched the shoulder of one next to them, including Notti. One by one their gemstones glowed like a string of Christmas tree lights.

"Wow," said Notti, as she watched the colorful sight against the background of the sky.

As if prompted by a symphony orchestra, the lightning exploded in a pattern across the sky. Shades of pink and blue embraced the rain clouds, and the wind howled mightily around the camp. Wara stood tall and nodded to the two women who had walked with her. They motioned to the children to stand and escorted them up the stone steps.

One by one girls and boys paraded across a platform in front of drummers, before standing behind a large flat stone. Wara raised her hand, and the drummers responded with a slow and rhythmic melody. A small man stepped forward and blew a clear and gentle tone from a large conch shell. The thunder boomed and the lightning shot through the sky, drowning out the shell's echo. More people appeared and gathered to form a semicircle around the platform. Notti noticed the calm and serene gazes on their faces as they all joined hands and closed their eyes.

Wara took Notti's hand and motioned to her to join hands with the girl next to her. Soon all the children had joined hands. The lightning struck several hundred feet away from the platform in an amazing display of jagged sparks. No one moved, but Notti felt her whole body tighten up. She squeezed Wara's hand and suddenly, Notti heard the whispering voice.

"Prepare yourself dream child, and do not be afraid.
    Your dream mother is here to guide and protect you."
Notti turned but saw no one else but the people who had gathered. Wara concentrated on the flat stone, while everyone continued their half talking and half singing with rising voices.

The thunder boomed again, and the air cooled down. Notti could hear the rain, but for some reason it stayed just outside of the camp and encircled them.

A streak of lightning hit the flat rock and sent it hurling up into the air. Notti tried to get up and run, but Wara held her hand firmly. She lifted her eyes to the flying stone as it soared higher. The stone burst into a whirlwind of small pieces, and the chorus of singers changed their pitch. They began harmonizing lower and lower. The thunder returned and the whirlwind of colors turned faster and faster. They came together and blended into a reddish-brown hue.

The color took form, and the form grew.

"I think I see a head and an arm," shouted Notti. "Look, it's a person," continued Notti while looking up at the spinning figure.

"But how can that be?" she asked as she lowered her voice.

The figure continued to spin, but slower now to reveal a beautiful woman with shoulder length dark hair. Her head tilted back, and her arms crossed over her chest. She floated down slowly until she bent over like a curled-up infant, just inches above the platform.

The rain turned into a gentle mist as the storm pulled away and headed to another destination. Notti watched two women rush to wrap the floating woman in a blue cloth. Gracefully she rose and stood suspended over an inch from the ground. Notti leaned over slightly to see that there was space between the lady and the ground. She wondered why, just as the lady spoke.

"It is unwise for me to touch the ground, for roots will form and bury themselves within the earth. I will forever remain here as a member of the plant kingdom. I serve my people best while afloat.”

Notti’s eyes widened and she wondered if the floating woman had read her mind.

 “Wait a minute, I understood what you said,” said Notti with renewed enthusiasm.

“We all speak one language now and share our thoughts,” said the lady.

Notti realized that everyone was looking at her. Shyly, she lowered her head as the lady spoke. “With love I thank you for calling me to this time and place. Chango, lord of thunder and lightning also thanks you.”

“You are welcome my dear May Ya,” replied Wara.

Everyone left the platform hand in hand with an entire procession of drummers, chanters, and children. They passed the woods and onto another campsite. Notti followed, amazed she could finally understand someone.

Not just anyone, but a lovely lady who emerged from a bolt of lightning and a whirlwind of a broken stone.

Chapter Sixteen

QUESTIONS AND ANSWERS

The long procession entered the camp near a large tree in the center. Lady May Ya greeted each person who came to pay their respects. Each time she bowed her head, her appearance would change into a new person. Notti watched in astonishment, while wondering how and why the lady would change to be someone else.

Notti felt a tap on her shoulder and turned to see a girl smiling at her.

"I'm ZinGa, what's your name?"
"I'm Notti."
"Hello Notti, do you know anybody else here?"
"No, I just got here today, how about you?"

"I arrived yesterday, but many others arrived two days before," said Zinga as she looked at Lady May Ya before she spoke again.

"She is lovely and gracious, do you agree?"

"Yes, she is," replied Notti. "But her face changes every time she talks to somebody else. One minute she looks younger and the next she looks older, and even her hair color changes. I've never seen anyone like her before."

"Zinga's eyes twinkled, and suddenly the line dispersed. Notti found herself and Zinga in the center of a large crowd.

"Gather around everyone so I may speak of the present time," announced Lady May Ya.

Most everyone sat towards the front of the platform. So, Notti and Zinga moved closer to the front and found a spot to sit together and listen.

"My time here is brief, so let us get to the matter at hand," began Lady May Ya.

"Many here have heard of how entry into the dreamtime portals may soon close for our young dreamers and light carriers. Especially if disbelief and doubt continue to penetrate the hearts and thoughts of the disenchanted, and.   If a disregard for the ancestors continues, we will lose our connection. It is vital for everyone to understand what is taking place, which is why we are gathered here today."

Notti looked at her bracelet and thought of Grandpa Pine. She looked around hoping he might be somewhere watching and listening to Lady May Ya, but sadly he wasn't.

"The dream portals are in danger," continued Lady May Ya.

"Ignorance as well as evil plots and deeds are being committed around the world to prevent the ancestors from communicating with their loved ones. As the ancestral guardian of the dream portal, I am asking you to be aware of those who may try to destroy what has always been practiced. You have been invited here for a specific task. This is because you have demonstrated to an ancestor your willingness to believe in the dreamtime."

Notti thought about the pirate dream and how glad she had felt to share it with Hanna, Aunt Lizzy, and Grandma Pine, who all believed her. Suddenly in that moment, it didn't matter where she was or when she'd get home, she knew this is where she was supposed to be.

"Many of you have already been advised on how you may help. I invite the recent arrivals to meet with me for their advice as well. My dear dreamers, we have an opportunity to help many transcend through time and space. We will also need to continue the sacred practice of carrying within us light and not stones."

Notti leaned over and whispered to Zinga.

"Are there more coming here?"

"No, not here, but to places all over the world. We must work together to keep the dream portals open. If not, then there will be no dream travel for anyone."

Notti nodded that she understood.

"Please close your eyes now and empty your mind of all things," continued Ma Ya.

"It is time to allow the uniting thought of peace to enter without interference."

Notti closed her eyes and concentrated on the little specks of color and light patterns under her eye lids. Curiosity crept in several seconds later, and she peeked out from one eye to see a beautiful golden glow radiating above them all. Not certain what the color meant, she hoped the glow signaled goodness and unity before closing her eye again.

"Thank you for inviting peace to reside within you," said Lady May Ya.

"Now I will speak to the newest children individually," she said looking at the attendants.

Notti opened her eyes and sighed heavily as she felt an overall calm come over her. Wara looked at Notti and smiled affectionately.

"It is time for any questions you may have to be answered. I'm happy to speak to you, and for that we can thank our special lady of time."

Notti returned Wara's smile.

"Thank you for taking care of me Wara," said Notti affectionately.

"You are welcome," replied Wara.

"Come with me now and you may speak with our lady."

Lady May Ya smiled as Notti approached her.

"Well, at last we meet and can speak to one another face to face," said Lady May Ya.

"Do you remember when I spoke to you in the plains and on the mountain?"

"That was you?"

"Yes, now please sit close to me," she said affectionally with her arms open for a hug.

They embraced and Notti looked into her brown eyes and saw her first-grade teacher, Sister Ann Marie, the nicest teacher at Saint Monica's.

Lady May Ya held Notti's face with both hands and looked into her eyes.

"You are a very brave girl to have traveled from such a great distance with the guidance and vision of your grandfather. You must love him very much."

"Yes, I do. How did you know that?"

"I know because it was me who asked your grandfather to send for you. It was me who sent messages to other light carriers to give you the gem of courage for your silver bracelet," replied Lady May Ya.

"Oh," said Notti, thinking of Hanna, Patrick, and Aunt Lizzy at the witch's tower.

"Wara was entrusted to bring you here safely," she continued. Notti asked, "was I in danger?"

Lady May Ya looked around the camp at all the children and adults quietly waiting, before answering.

"The ancestors were concerned you might arrive in the middle of a border attack between two opposing tribes."

"Yes, I saw one, and it was terrible," said Notti recalling the painted men.

"The men, who found you, were a patrol sent by Wara. We are thankful they found you." Notti looked at her curiously, wondering how she could look so much like her favorite teacher before asking her anything.

"Why am I here?"

"Let's begin with your bracelet. It is very old and has been on the wrists of many young men and women before you. The bracelet serves as a conduit for several kinds of good power when aligned with a gem and a vision. Power can be useful but can be equally dangerous when used improperly. You are here to meet me and to receive the gem scroll of definitions for your bracelet. When you return home, you will learn how to use your gems with the guidance of your mentor."

Notti looked at her bracelet and ran her finger over the two gems.

"What kinds of things will I learn?"

"Too many things for me to explain now. Trust that what you do learn will be important for the future of the dreamtime."

"Oh," said Notti as her curiosity rose.

"You must learn and practice until you build your confidence and skills. Remember to never take your bracelet off, and to travel with the memory of your grandfather. Use what you've learned wisely."

"How come I traveled when I fell asleep? It doesn't make any sense to me," said Notti as she shook her head in confusion.

There was a soft gasp from the handful waiting their turn. Notti realized from their looks she had spoken disrespectfully.

"Things won't make sense when you are not familiar with them," said Lady May Ya with a little sternness in her voice and a reassuring pat on Notti's back. Notti thought again of Aunt Lizzy's advice and the story of the astronomer.

"You may travel whether you are awake or asleep, but until you master the gems, asleep is the most effective way to begin."

"Please tell me why," said Notti, as she hung on to her every word.

"When you're awake, you are more prone to the distraction of the journey. You may lose the vision of your guide, or your grandfather, and miss the dream portal. If that should happen, you could be thrust into a place and time where you have no ancestral or governing guidance. This may leave you at a risk of being stranded."

" Oh, you mean no one might know me there," said Notti.

"Yes, and that is why keeping your grandfather within your memory of him is so crucial to your dreamtime education."

"Okay," said Notti as she nodded with a better understanding.

"You will leave here for your home after the closing ceremony, and Elizabeth, or Aunt Lizzy will be your mentor. She will teach you well, so listen to her and always do your best, so that when we call, you will be ready."

"Really, Aunt Lizzy is my mentor?"

"Yes, of course, and she is delighted, as you will help her to introduce Hanna to the practice as well."

"But she's not one of my ancestors, so how can she be my mentor?"

"Notti, the dreamtime is not owned by a specific race or continent, and there are many who acknowledge the relationship between mortals and ancestors. This practice is above differences. It is a uniting practice for those who desire to communicate and be guided by their loved ones unconditionally. Now go in peace knowing that many others including your grandfather are there for you always," said Lady May Ya while squeezing Notti affectionately.

Notti felt warmth and a wave of what seemed like electricity travel through her. She sighed gratefully for the attention.

"Okay, thank you," said Notti as May Ya let her go.

Wara extended her graceful hand to help Notti. Together they walked past the line of eager children to a small grass hut. Wara stepped inside with Notti, and they sat down together.

"I still don't understand a few things," said Notti.

"Understanding takes patience and constant learning, my child. Someday you will understand more, but for now you must take one step at a time," said Wara.

"I guess I just don't know anything. This is all so new, and what about my parents?"

Wara patted Notti's back and gently spoke.

"Have no fear my child, for you will be a good student. I cannot explain everything but know that you are here for a good reason. Your family will not experience your absence, for the dreamtime is timeless. You will leave here, but your lessons will continue with the mentor from your home just as our Lady said. You have been through quite a bit already," continued Wara. Notti shrugged her shoulders and nodded before replying.

"Yeah, and did the men from your village tell you about the giant snake?" Wara nodded.

"You were most fortunate to have Serpent Ura come to rescue you. She is a most powerful ancestor, and she will protect you in any body of water."

Notti's eyebrows rose as she pondered how a serpent could protect her. Wara saw her reaction and smiled.

"You have ancestor assistants in the elemental worlds of plants, water, and fire. And you also have mammal and reptilian guides"

"Oh," said Notti not sure how to respond.

"Where did Lady May Ya come from?" asked Notti curiously.

"I was taught as a child that she came to us from a star. She came to earth and entered the sea and dwelt with the dolphins and the whales. She then came to shore and presented herself to the mountain people of this land. She is of pure light and can replicate any female likenesses familiar to whomever she addresses. She holds great knowledge and is here to help us."

"Why do we need help?"

Wara shifted her weight so she could sit closer. Notti could feel a story coming, so she also made herself comfortable.

"Through-out the world, we have heard of alarming occurrences. This has resulted in a dramatic change in the belief and practice of reverence for our natural world. The relationship between man and the natural world is threatened. The ancestors have requested several summits to the governing lords and ladies of the elemental and physical world. You are at this moment participating in a summit at a region once known as Mu Land."

Notti's ears perked up at the name, and her thoughts raced back to Patrick's magazine. She wondered if it could be true that such a place once existed?

"Notti, this gathering is to help resolve the occurrences which could potentially abolish an ancient system. In many areas of the world there is a growing disbelief in the relationship between family members in the present, and with family who have passed on. For example, just north of here is the city of Zaga, with a powerful river we call Oshun. Lady Oshun is the love and healing force of that river. She gives life to the land by overflowing the river each year to help make the land fertile and healthy. The crops grow abundantly, and the people are then filled with good health, fertility, love of life, prosperity, and joy."

"I never heard of a river having a life," said Notti.

"Life is also another word for energy, which can take on form within the natural elements of air, fire, water, and earth. Everything has energy," said Wara.

"Oh," said Notti, remembering what Aunt Lizzy said about how magic couldn't be explained.

Lady Oshun has disappeared," continued Wara.

"The local farmers and villagers are fearful that they will starve without her to flood the land with fertile silt. Because of this they are over harvesting the fish and crossing over peaceful boundaries to take more than they need of crops. Villagers are convinced that the natural and ancestral world has abandoned them. Without their belief in our ancestors, communications and the ability to travel within the dreamtime portals will close. The teachings of our relationship with the natural world will be lost or be gone with our elders."

Notti sighed and thought of her grandpa's disappointment with her father for not wanting to learn about their ancestors or about natural energy.

Wara continued. "Although, there are similar occurrences around the world, there are several gathered here today who want to help find Lady Oshun. Like you dear Notti, the other children are also here to begin their lessons of the dreamtime."

"Wow, that's amazing that I will learn about the dreamtime, and that you think I can help," said Notti. She now held genuine enthusiasm to do her best to make her grandfather proud. proud.

Chapter Seventeen

LADY MAY YA' S GIFT

A gathering for the joyous feast and a bountiful ceremony had begun. Conga drummers beat a deep alto rhythm, and percussionists playing cow bells and beaded gourds. Dancers jumped high in an energetic musical circle. Others sang along as they watched and ate from a diverse buffet. Notti searched through the crowd for Zinga and finally found her standing near a large and colorful spread of platters and bowls of food.

"Hi," said Zinga handing Notti a bowl.

"Hi," said Notti looking curiously at all the food.

"That is camel meat," said Zinga pointing to the largest platter.

"Oh," said Notti trying not to look too squeamish. "What does it taste like?" she asked, as Zinga spooned up a generous helping for herself.

"To me it tastes like a young cow, but a little sweeter. Would you like to try some?"

"Yes please," said Notti, as her stomach grumbled.

"Over here is water lily with snails, and this is porridge with goat milk and dried shrimp."

"Oh," said Notti, eager to try everything.

"This is river fish with root vegetables, and in the corner are dates," concluded Zinga.

"Wow, I've never eaten food like this before," said Notti with renewed enthusiasm.

Zinga handed her the porridge spoon and Notti helped herself to a generous portion.

"I think I'll pass on the snails though and go for the dates," said Notti politely.

"Eat whatever you like, it's all good," said Zinga.

They found a place to sit in the shade behind the platform. Notti took a healthy bite of the camel meat and gleefully replied.

"You're right it does taste like veal."

"What is veal?" asked Zinga.

"That's what we call baby cow meat," said Notti chewing slowly and enjoying the different flavors and textures on her palate.

"Did you have a nice talk with Lady May Ya?" asked Zinga.
"Yes, I suppose so. She helped me to understand a little more about why I'm here. Did you come here by yourself too?"
"No, I came with an escort arranged by my family."
"Your family arranged for you to come here?"
Zinga nodded before taking another bite of her porridge.
"Wow, my parents don't know anything about where I am," said Notti.
"Your grandpa knows where you are," said Zinga.

Notti was just about to ask how she knew about Grandpa, when Wara came from the crowd.

"Notti, I must attend to May Ya's needs before the ceremony. Stay close to the platform so I may find you afterwards," she said while prancing off.
Notti looked at Zinga curiously before asking.
"Do you know what ceremony Wara is talking about?"
"Yes, the ceremony will take place on the platform, and Lady May Ya will give us the gem of guidance and protection before she departs," replied Zinga.
"Will we be in the ceremony too?" asked Notti, as she adjusted her wrap around her belly.
"Yes, we will receive her gifts and give her our word that we will complete our tasks."
"You have a task?"
"Yes, I am to go to the great kingdom of Dongo and meet with the royal prince. He may have knowledge of Lady Oshun's disappearance," replied Zinga.
"You're going to meet with a real prince?"
"Well, yes because I am also from a royal family, and Lady May Ya believes it will be easier for me to gain entrance without any suspicion."
"Wow, you're a princess or something?"
"Yes," whispered Zinga. "It is best to keep it between us," she said casually.

"Oh," said Notti not wanting to pry any further, but instead share her own task.

"I'm to study with my mentor back home and learn more about the dreamtime. I haven't heard of Dongo before, but when I get home, I'll look it up at the library or see if I can learn more at the history museum.

"What is a museum?" asked Zinga.

Notti looked at her as if she were a little nutty.

"You don't know what a museum is?"
"No," she replied.

"Well, it's a building where you can go and see things that have been researched, found, or dug up from different cultures and places. You know things like dinosaur bones and artifacts." Zinga looked at Notti a little closer, and then her eyes lit up.

"You're from the future!"
"What are you talking about? What do you mean the future?" asked Notti.
"You are not from this time. You came from another time," said Zinga.
"Well what time is this?" asked Notti.

Zinga chuckled and shook her head. "That is why your words are so amusing."

Notti frowned as Zinga continued to chuckle and reply.

"This is the time of the great migration to Mu Land, one the volcanic islands."

Stunned, Notti thought about it and scratched her head, as she looked at Zinga doubtfully.

"Where are these islands?"

"They are far west from here. There is talk of a wealth of minerals to be mined, and so many are leaving to start a new life there."

"Oh, well that's good I suppose, but it must be hard for people to leave their home and move to some place far away and different," said Notti sadly.

"Yes, but because the fertile farmlands are drying up, many will have to give up being farmers and become miners and traders."

"Oh," said Notti as she finished her porridge and sighed with satisfaction.

"I was wondering if you go to school," said Notti.

"I have tutors in astronomy, writing, and philosophy," said Zinga as she set down her bowl.

"Wow! That sounds interesting. We're studying American history in school right now."

"What is American History?" asked Zinga.

"It's the story of the country I come from," said Notti suddenly stunned before asking her.

"Wow, I have traveled back in time!"

Zinga tapped Notti's arm, fearing she had caused Notti to go into shock.

"I hope you are not upset," she said with a genuine concern.

Notti swallowed hard and took several deep breaths.

"Oh no, I'm fine. I should have known better, especially since a couple of nights ago I was on a pirate ship."

Zinga nodded and tried to understand before replying.

"I have never been to your time through the dream portals," she whispered.
"Oh," said Notti again, not wanting to appear anymore ignorant than she already felt.
"What is it like where you are from?" asked Zinga.
"Well, we don't have princes and princesses, and we don't have parties like this."
Zinga nodded and asked, "who governs you then?"

Notti explained the system of government as best she could. How most families had celebrations with sit down dinner parties, or birthday parties for their children. Zinga listened attentively to Notti's every word. Just like a toddler listening to her mother's instructions.

The girls talked until Wara returned and tapped Notti on the shoulder.

"It's time for the ceremony. Please sit with the rest of the children in front of the platform."

"Wara, I just found out that I'm here from the future. Am I the only one?"

"Yes, Notti you are, and you will learn to summon others from the future with whom you know and trust when you travel back again."

Notti nodded and watched Wara walk briskly away.

"This is really amazing," said Notti as she and Zinga stood up.
"I agree. You are the first person from the future I have ever met," said Zinga.

They found a place to sit in front of the platform. While they waited, Notti marveled again at the many people. All in bold colorful tunics, beaded vests, and varied hair styles. Some wore braided hair designs. others were shaven bald with designs on their temples. Many bowed their heads in greetings to Notti and Zinga as they passed by. Notti felt gratitude bubbling inside of her like a shaken and opened can of soda pop.

A drum roll sounded, and all the children made their way to the platform. Together they watched Lady May Ya float down onto the center of the platform.

The cool and steady mountain breeze brushed against Lady May Ya. Making her thick hair dance about her head like a lion's mane. An elderly man stood humbly next to her. He held a large wooden bowl filled with small animal skin bags. When everyone had settled, Lady May Ya spoke with a booming and clear voice.

"I am thankful to all of you for your presence here today. I am equally thankful for this opportunity to speak to you, and for you to speak to one another."

Notti heard behind her the rain and the thunder. She kept her attention on listening to Lady May Ya.

"In this large bowl are small bags filled with the gems of light. Several of you children already have a gem or two, or a bag of the remaining gems. For those who don't you will receive the remaining gems. With these you will learn to use them under the guidance of your mentor.

Dear children of light, use your abilities wisely. Do not darken your light with arrogance, greed, envious competition, or judgment. Draw upon courage for important decisions."

The wind picked up, carrying with it the scent of rain. In the distance the clouds grew darker but stayed away. It was as if waiting for the appropriate moment to arrive. Wara and another woman passed out the bags according to an embroidered symbol. Wara handed Notti a leather wristband and told her to wear it over her bracelet, so that no attention would be drawn to it. Notti leaned over to see that Zing's bag had a diamond shape symbol on it. When the bags were all handed out, Lady May Ya continued. "There is much work to be done and no time to waste. Do not underestimate the power you hold on to your wrists, nor the power you hold in your hearts. Power can easily work for you as well as against you, so be careful.

"Each gem color represents a unique ability," said Lady May Ya.

"Know that the most important abilities come from the red gem for portal travel and the green gem for communication."

Notti covered her bracelet with the wrist band, and the other children hung their bags of gems around their necks.

While holding Wara's hand, Lady May Ya gestured for everyone to join hands. She raised herself a little higher off the platform. The crowd watched as the storm clouds encircled the group, and thunder sounded off its powerful voice. May Ya shouted out her final instructions.

"To communicate with me, simply touch the red garnet gem. Envision with clarity of mind and purity of heart what you need or are asking.   I will hear you. Be careful of your special gifts and do not use them to court evil. For it will enslave you. Go now in peace, embrace your lessons, and serve your mission well."   The accelerated rumbling of the storm and lightning struck behind her with a flash. Notti trembled as a strange sensation rippled through her body. Thunder boomed and May Ya rose even higher. Tearfully, Wara watched her lady rise slowly into the gathering storm just as a loud cry rang through the crowd.

Everyone turned to see over a half dozen men run into the camp, swinging wood rods high above their heads, and yelling, "Don't move, we've got you now!"

Chapter Eighteen

ATTACK OF THE KERMAS

"Run Notti, run to Wara, it's the Kerma slave traders," screamed Zinga. She ran into the forest in search of her mentor. Notti stood stunned for a moment in disbelief as adults ran to grab children, while many others scattered in every direction.

"Grab the young and able adults. Do away with the old," yelled a Kerma.

Notti looked to Wara just as another Kerma ran up to the platform.

"Stop that creature," he yelled. Lady May Ya hung suspended over the platform waiting for Lord Chango of thunder to come for her. A trader swung a whip into a lasso around May Ya's legs and pulled her down.

"Release me," she bellowed as she opened her hand and spread her fingers to ignite a shooting flame from her fingertips. The engulfed whip sent a trail of fire to the trader's fist. He screamed and dropped the whip to cradle his hand.

"Children of Light, I cannot help you now," cried May Ya. " I will be watching over you and will receive your message when you call upon me."

She spun up like a beam of light through an opening in the storm clouds and disappeared as it closed in on her. Notti watched the scene in horror just as she heard Wara's voice above the commotion.

"Notti, I'm behind the platform, hurry!"

"Wara, Wara, I'm coming," yelled Notti, running in-between and through the panic.

As she reached the platform, a Kerma ran up from behind. He grabbed her and threw her over his shoulder as Wara watched helplessly.

"Be brave Notti," she yelled. The delighted Kerma carried Notti off through the dispersing crowd. Notti lifted her head as far as she could in time to see Wara stretch her arms over three children, and instantly together they disappeared.

"Wara, come back, don't leave me here", cried Notti. She tried to kick herself free, but the Kerma held her down with a firm grip.

"Let me go! Put me down," screamed Notti. She hung over him on her belly like a sack of potatoes.

He ran out of the camp past the frightened and fleeing. The up and down motion upset Notti's full stomach, and she heaved, throwing up everything as they continued on. She moaned at the taste of stomach acid coating her mouth.

"Help me, I need water," she blurted out.
"Shut up and stop your vomiting," shouted the Kerma as he slowed to a walk. Another Kerma ran up alongside him, laughing and slapping his thigh.

"Hey YuBa, you got the sickly runt. You can't demand a good price if there's nothing left of her. Better hunting next time," he said laughing and running off for a captive.

YuBa grunted but said nothing. Notti felt weak draped over his shoulder. While watching the beaten ground beneath her, YuBa stopped. He dropped Notti into the arms of another trader before running off to hunt for another.

"You will bring a good price," said the trader as he tied her arms behind her and forced her to kneel behind him and wait. Notti watched and trembled as more captives were tied and bound together. There were several other children. Notti realized the rest must have found their mentors and disappeared.

"Why did I wait? I should have run as soon as Zinga said to," she thought, as she regrettably shook her head. A boy tied and sitting in front of Notti turned and whispered consoling words.

"Try not to worry. If there is a chance for me to help you, I will. My name is BurK, and I will be your friend." Notti sniffed and nodded.

"Thank you BurK," she managed to say with a glimmer of hope.

Time passed by slowly as the Kermas continued to tie everyone they had captured.

YuBa and others eventually returned. YuBa walked back and forth with his hands on his hips and looked sternly at the huddled captives. Notti trembled at his scowl and piercing black eyes. His large pointed and bumpy nose reminded her of a vulture's beak.

Pleased with his count he smiled, revealing stained and missing teeth. He paused for a moment before cracking his whip on the ground and stirring up a small cloud of dirt.

"Get up and form a line," he growled like a wild beast. With her hands tied, Notti struggled to stand up behind BurK. She let out a small gasp when she saw his tied hands dripping of blood down to the back of his legs. He heard her and whispered.

"I'm alright. It doesn't hurt anymore."

A Kerma strung a rope through each of their arms to keep them in line. They were forced to walk around the wounded who cried out in pain. Notti burst into tears when she saw the old woman who had braided her hair lying on the ground barely alive. Notti tried to stop. She wanted to help, to touch her, to whisper a kind word, and to do anything to give her some reassurance.

"Move along you, and get back in line," yelled a Kerma to Notti.
"Let us go, we have done nothing wrong," pleaded the woman.
"Let us return to our homes and families," begged another.
"Shut your mouths and do what you are told," said YuBa with his menacing eyes.

Notti looked away and lowered her head.

"Be grateful you were not struck down like others," laughed a Kerma as the captives were led down the mountain trail.

That night the captives all settled down in a camp not far from the base of the mountain. There were no grass huts, no goat skins, and no straw mats. They were ordered to form a circle and find a spot on the ground. The long rope was released, and they were told they would be fed in the morning. Notti knelt and tried to get comfortable. Closing her eyes, she thought of Grandpa Pine and wondered if he knew where she was. He would help her get home, she thought over and over again. Soon she fell asleep and into her dreams, and the first to appear was Grandpa Pine.

He stood in front of the Witch's Tower looking up at her and shaking his head and his index finger. Notti looked down and found she was sitting on a small cloud floating just above him. She opened her mouth to speak, but nothing came out. Grandpa pointed to his ear, and although he didn't open his mouth, she suddenly heard him.

"Notti, my darling girl, listen carefully as I send you my thought message."

"Okay," Notti heard herself say without opening her mouth as well.

"I want you to take this unfortunate situation and use it to help rescue Lady Oshun.
 I know where she is hidden, and I will help you. I will come back for you, so don't worry darling girl, I believe in you."

Grandpa Pine faded and finally disappeared, as did the tower and the hill. Notti opened her eyes to find herself still curled up next to the other sleeping captives. She felt tears mounting but fought them back. She trusted her grandpa, and she felt assured he would return.

The days that followed began with the crack of a whip at sunrise. They were fed small portions of dry flat bread and a drink of water. Later they would stop to relieve themselves. Again, they were tied and roped back together before being forced to walk through cold mountain springs, harsh dry lands, and thick grassy fields until sunset.

Along the way Notti observed how the Kerma's knew exactly when to stop, how long everyone should rest, and how much water and food to give to each captive. The only other people they saw on the route were other traders on camels or on horses, carrying large bundles of goods and supplies. The traders exchanged words about the weather and warnings of thieves on the trail. Occasionally, they would inspect and give comments about the apparent value and worth of each captive.

One night the caravan camped near another camp of traders. The Kermas took the ropes off and gave the usual small rations of bread and water. Soon everyone began to fall asleep. Notti listened to her stomach growl for more food. She thought of all the times she hadn't finished her greasy fish sticks, dry meatloaf, or overcooked liver with onions that Mom served.

"What I would do for a plate of Mom's home cooking right now," she thought rubbing her empty tummy, as she listened to a trader.

"The queen's soldiers are capturing and buying any and all slaves," she heard one trader say.
"There is talk of a new palace to be built in honor of the queen in Dongo," said another.
Notti's ears perked up at the mention of Dongo, and she thought of Zinga.
"The young king will need builders, grounds keepers, artisans and maids to attend to his mother and sister as well," said another trader.

"Good news, for we will have plenty to sell, and we know where to find more," said YuBa.

"It will take many more days to complete this palace, which means many days of good trading for us," he concluded. The men laughed and nodded in agreement. Notti continued to listen as they went on and on about their plans for the gold they would receive at the slave market.

"I'm going to be sold like an animal at a market", thought Notti. "If the king buys me, what will he have me do?"

Her mind raced with questions and fears, but then she remembered Wara's last words, and she knew she had to figure a way out.

The wind kicked up the sand and Notti thought about waking up and warning the others, but already they were stirring and positioning themselves away from the wind. She turned around to shield herself, and that is when she saw a large snake burying itself in the sand. The gust heightened, and with it came a strange whispering voice.

"Do not let fear embrace you. Use the gem to summon someone you trust."

The voice sounded calm, and Notti felt an immediate ease as if she were listening to an old friend.

"It must be the serpent ancestor," she thought as the gust stopped, and the air settled. She didn't have to think long or hard about a person, because Patrick came to her mind first. She wondered if he would help her again.

The traders had fallen asleep, and only the watchman stood leaning up against a post, nodding occasionally in and out of sleep.

Notti lay on her side and pulled the wrist band off slightly to peek at her bracelet. She touched the garnet gem and envisioned Lady MayYa before making her request. She pictured Patrick and whispered her plea.

"Patrick, I'm in the past and the slave traders are holding me prisoner. Please help me escape," she murmured it over and over again until she fell asleep from the day's exhaustion.

Chapter Nineteen

TO MARKET

"Wake up now," yelled the Kerma with the large belly and shifty eyes.

He pointed to three wagons, and three horses parked near a cluster of boulders.

"Into the wagons," he continued to shout. "We'll reach the city before mid-day, so on your feet! No time for food, your new masters will feed you soon enough."

Another Kerma passed the water bag down the line while two other Kermas slipped ropes over each captive's head. Notti stood and stretched out her kinks from the hard night's sleep on the ground. She was handed the water bag from which she took a long drink. The dryness of the night air had left her thirsty, and the water tasted better than a root beer soda on a summer's day.

As she turned to pass on the bag, she realized she was the last one in line. The night guard ran over to take it from her. Even though his head and face was covered, Notti noticed something familiar about his eyes.

He squinted, looked cautiously from side to side, and then unexpectedly clamped his hand over Notti's mouth. Notti tried to wiggle free from his hand, but he gripped her face tightly while putting a finger to his lips.

"Don't say a word. Listen, and do what I say," he whispered.

"Get down on your belly and crawl to the sand drifts behind you. Then run and count to fifty until you reach the sand dunes. Hide and I'll find you," he said moving his hand away.

Notti's mouth dropped open and asked. "Patrick?"

He nodded and pushed her down, while a few captives immediately bunched up to shield her escape. Notti scurried on her belly towards the tall grass and never looked back.

"He's here, he's here", was all she could think of as relief suddenly released her stress.

"What's going on down there? Get those people back in line," ordered a trader.

Patrick pulled out his whip and cracked it near the feet of the captives, as he turned to watch Notti quickly crawl away.

"Get back in line, you heard him. Come on move it!"

Notti continued to crawl on her belly and pull herself through the sand. Sand filled her tunic and irritated her skin with every crawl until her knees felt raw. She had to take a chance. So up she stood and ran just as Patrick climbed on to a horse and pulled back on the reins.

"Someone's trying to escape," shouted Patrick. A Kerma cursed and ran for a horse.

"I'll get her," continued Patrick as he took off in a gallop.

"Don't beat her. No bruises and no exposed cuts," shouted the Kerma.

Notti ran, panting and counting, forty-eight, forty-nine, fifty. Seeing a large sand dune, she dove behind it to wait. Her heart pounded and sweat trickled down the side of her face.

"It's Patrick, it's really him," she said out of breath. Lady MayYa must have sent him," she thought, wiping her forehead with her tunic sleeve. She heard galloping and anxiously waited.

"Notti, Notti, where are you?" called Patrick as he steered the horse around the dunes.

Notti stood up just as Patrick came into view. Seeing Notti, he pulled up on his reins, then removed his mask and spoke.

"We have to get you out of here. Ride and sit behind me and hold on. Can you do that?"

"Yes, I guess so. Why, is it hard to do?"

"Not if you sit close and move when I do. The slave traders are going to get suspicious and send someone after me, so we've got to go. Here, I'll help you up."

Patrick reached down, and Notti grabbed his hands.

And with all his strength, Patrick pulled her up. Notti let out a grunt as she threw her leg over the horse and sat on the blanket.

"Wow, you're pretty strong," she said as she inched up and threw her arms around his waist.

"Thanks, I do sit-ups and push-ups every day," he said with a slight blush.

"I've got to get you to Dongo, and the best way to do that is to ride ahead of the Kermas and then get back on the trail. So, hold on tight."

"What? Take me to Dongo?

Let's just go home because this place is crazy. These people are cruel and dangerous. If Mom ever found out what I just went through, she'd never let me dreamtime travel again," she said while holding on.

"I'm sorry Notti. I can't take you home; only your grandpa can do that. I think he wants you to stay, because I was told to take you to Dongo, so are you ready or not"?

At the mention of her grandfather, she fell silent. She let out a deep sigh and looked at the miles upon miles of sand stretching out before them. The intense heat beat down upon her, and she thought of how wonderful a shower would feel right now.

"Okay, I'm ready," she whispered.

"Okay," said Patrick. "Once we are past the Kermas, we'll take another route just above them. It's a little longer, but at least they won't be following us because we'll be behind them."

Patrick leaned over to the horse's ear.

"Lightning, mighty horse, carry us to our destination", whispered Patrick.

"You're talking to the horse?"

Patrick didn't answer because Lightning took off at a fast trot. First making its way around the dunes, and then into a full gallop atop the packed sand. Notti turned her head from the wind as the dust blew across her face. She squinted at the sun and held on tightly to Patrick, while mighty Lightening moved with incredible speed and grace.

Notti felt lightness as if they were flying across the land to the rhythm of each gallop. They raced through colors and landscapes that most people only see in photographs or magazines. The enormous blue sky, the long and distant horizon, and the bright blazing sun all raced by.

"Look to your right," shouted Patrick, while pulling tightly on the reins to hold Lightning and keep him from bolting. Notti turned to see a dark cloud moving towards them. As the cloud moved closer, they heard the galloping roar of over thirty wild horses pounding across their path.

"Wow, I've never seen so many horses before," shouted Notti while coughing up dust before burying her head into Patrick's back with gratitude.

He had come to rescue her. For the first time since her arrival to the clay village she felt confident that Grandpa Pine and now Lady MayYa were truly watching over her. The horses disappeared into the sunrise and Lightning continued to race across the sand like a fired bullet.

The landscape blurred, and Notti was reminded of the day she left for her new neighborhood. She thought of the tower, the mysterious winged people, and of everything she experienced since her arrival at Mu land. She thought of Zinga and the rest of the light children with their dreamtime bracelets, and she wondered if she would ever see them again. And now here she was escaping from Kermas with her dreamtime friend Patrick.

They rode towards the northeast until Patrick steered Lightning back onto the trail. Notti felt hungry and tired all at once, and shortly there afterwards, Patrick pulled up slowly on the reins until Lightning walked before coming to a stop. Notti could see palm trees in the distance, and for a moment wondered if it could be a mirage.

"We're not far from the Oshun River," said Patrick as he jumped off and helped Notti down.

"Even though we took a longer route, you're almost to Dongo.

Patrick grabbed the water bag and handed it to her. "You look hot. You should drink something," he said kindly.

"There's a small creek over there, and I'm going to take Lightning there to get a drink. I'll be right back," he said pulling on the reins and leading the mighty beast away.

Notti took several gulps and breathed deeply as thoughts of the past continued to race through her mind. She thought of how Lady MayYa came from a rain cloud, and she replayed the brutal attack. She had witnessed sad and frightening things she never imagined, and she wondered what more could happen.

Patrick returned and took a swig of water from the bag. Notti could see that he was equally hot from his red cheeks and beaded brow. She suddenly felt secure about returning home and knowing that Patrick had traveled safely to her.

"I'll take you to the border of Dongo where others will help you," said Patrick.

"How do you know all this Patrick? I don't understand how you know so much."

"Well, I did get my dreamtime bracelet and put my gem in the bezel, and last night I had a dream about my great-grandmother. She told me to help you. She told me where you were and where to take you. I woke up and I was in the desert next to where you camped. It happened just like when you were in trouble on the pirate ship. I had a dream of Great-grandma Jones, and she told me what to do. When I lost you in the water after we escaped from the pirate ship, I never thought I'd see you again. But then when I saw you in school, I didn't know what to say."

"I didn't know what to say either. I thought you'd think I was crazy if I thanked you for helping me," said Notti shyly.

Patrick smiled and blushed at the compliment. He looked down at his feet to hide his shyness. Notti noticed, and wished she had the courage to hug him.

"I'm not sure why this is happening to me either," said Patrick as he shrugged his shoulders.

"All I know is that when I was little, I used to see things, and luckily, I could tell my dad. We were always close, and he always shared his dreams with me; especially when they were strange, or crazy dreams. He said that I would learn why I have dreams and how to use this gift."

"What's the gift?" asked Notti as her curiosity rose.

"My dad said that when you can see into another world, it's a gift. He said that our world and the dream world live together, but not everyone wants to see it."

"Do you think that the ancestors are ghosts?" continued Notti.

"I don't know, but I don't think we're supposed to be afraid of them, especially if they're related to us," said Patrick as he looked into Notti's brown eyes.

"We're probably here because of your grandfather and my great-grandmother. I think they're helping us to learn how to be better people," said Patrick as he mounted Lightening.

"We really need to get going," he said in a more serious tone.

Notti sighed and asked. "Did you know your great-grandmother?"

"I knew her when I was little. Mostly I remember her from the pictures. My mom says she really loved me and was so happy she lived long enough to see me," concluded Patrick.

Patrick reached for Notti's hand to help her up. Notti threw her leg over Lightening and wrapped her arms around Patrick's waist and rested her head on his back.

They rode with a light trot towards the palm trees. Notti looked at the land and a sudden feeling of belonging came over her. For some reason, this place began to have meaning, and she felt she had been here before.

Patrick kicked Lightning with his heels and the beast sped up into a steady gallop. They saw no one along the way. Neither camps nor villages were visible within the blended landscape. Notti was impressed with how well Patrick managed Lightning. She was beginning to think that he could do almost anything.

They rode until Patrick pulled up again on the reins to slow Lightning to a walk before finally stopping. He slid off and handed the reins to Notti.

"The sun is almost over you now. Keep riding east, and you will be at the village when the sun is right over your head. You're really close."

"You're leaving me? Why are you leaving?"
"I only came to help you get away from the Kermas," said Patrick.
"Why, who decided that?
"You did. Besides, I think I am just a helper. "Kind of like an elf."
"You're an elf? Is that why the pirates called you a pygmy?"

"I don't know why anyone would call me that, I'm not that short," he said somewhat embarrassed. When you get back home, I'll tell you what I learned from my great-grandmother and my dad. Then maybe you'll understand why I can't stay."

Notti nodded her and thought that nothing still made any sense, not one thing.

"I don't know how to ride a horse by myself. You can't go," she said searching for another reason for Patrick to stay.

"Don't worry because Lightning will know where to go. All you have to do is hold the reins and then pull on them when you want him to stop".

Notti looked at Lightning with some reservation, as she wondered how a horse would know where to go. Patrick held Lightning's head still in his hands and gently spoke to him.

"Take Notti down into the village. You belong to her now, and you must obey her wishes and commands." He kissed Lightning on the center of his forehead and stepped back to look at Notti.

"He will take you as far as he can. When you don't need him anymore, tell him to return to Lady MayYa, and if later you need him again, just call his name and he will come. Okay?"

"Okay," said Notti, with again some reservation. Having never had an animal of any kind before, she felt reluctant to take charge.

"Goodbye Notti and good luck."

"How are you going to get back," asked Notti with a look of concern.

Patrick pulled back the sleeve of his tunic revealing ahis silver bracelet with one gemstone.

"Remember the woman in the red cape from the Witch's Tower?"

"Yes, it was Aunt Lizzy," said Notti.

"Well, she gave me a gem too," said Patrick.

"If you got a gem, then how come you didn't come to the summit I went to?"

"I don't know, but I did go near the Mu land mountains, and I met a bunch of people."

Notti sighed and asked.

"Why did you go there?"

"I'm not sure, but I think it was to meet my ancestors."

"Wow, really?"

"Yeah, and they were really different."

"How were they different?"

Patrick hummed and hawed, looked down at his feet, and shrugged his shoulders.

"It's kind of hard to explain. How about if I tell you when you get back? Maybe then I'll know how to explain it. Besides, I should really get going so you can do what you're supposed to do."

"If you can get back with your gem, I should be able to get back too," she said defiantly.

"I don't think it works that way Notti. I think your grandpa has to make the decision for you to travel through the portal. You need to ask him."

"Okay," said Notti feeling defeated.

"Goodbye Notti."

"Goodbye Patrick and thank you for rescuing me again," she said with a smile.

"You're welcome, Notti. See ya back in Tangle Town."

They waved to each other until Notti turned toward the east.

"It's time to stop worrying," she told herself. The words were in her head, and she recited them over and over again, but still she felt a little frightened. Looking back once more she hoped to see Patrick on the trail, but he was gone. Only the dry land blanketed with patches of tall grass and dotted by flat-top trees remained.

Chapter Twenty

PRINCE TUTHRA & PRINCESS

ZINGA

Soon the land changed from sand and dust to green pockets of life quenched by mist and the morning dew. Alone for the first time in a land that both accepted and threatened her, Notti thought of Lady May Ya. She wondered if she could learn enough to help save the dreamtime portals. She also wondered how a girl from the future could be of any help to kings, princesses, farmers, and mystical ladies and lords.

As she bounced up and down on Lightning, her mind raced again through the days and

nights since she left Tangle Town. Never would she have imagined such a journey could happen to her. Soon people appeared on foot and on camels and horses. No one took much notice of Notti, except for those carrying heavy bundles.

"They're probably wondering why I have a horse, and they don't," she whispered to herself with a bit of guilt.

At long last, Notti rode up to the edge of a plateau and pulled on the reigns to stop Lightning. She looked down upon what looked like an ancient village spread out like an enormous lotus flower. Houses of clay and stone lined the river, and near the shore sat a magnificent clay palace with gardens, fields of grain, and herds of cattle.

Everywhere were people in the fields, on the dirt paths, and on the river in paddling canoes. Notti sat in complete awe of the scene. She did not realize that she and Lightning were blocking the path until someone began to complain.

"There now child, move along so we may be on our way," said a young woman carrying a bundle on her head. Notti snapped out of her gaze, took a deep breath, and quickly gave Lightning a nudge.

"Let's go Lightning," she called out.

Notti rode along the much-traveled path, and the closer she got to the village center the more people she passed. She came upon a large crowd patrolled by several soldiers mounted on camels. They wore white tunics, held long swords, and their bushy hair hung to their shoulders. One made eye contact with her, and a surge of panic-struck Notti as he hastened toward her. His stare felt penetrating and griped her anxious stomach like a squeezed sponge. She couldn't breathe and she dared not try to get away, especially with the large sword hanging from his hip.

"Halt," yelled the soldier.

Notti pulled on the reins and froze. With a pounding heart and a sudden surge of nausea and dizziness, she watched the soldier grab her reins. Suspiciously, he looked first at her tattered dusty clothes and then at her soiled face, but to her surprise he respectfully bowed his head.

"Are you Princess Notti from the land west of the great Oshun?"
"Ah, ah, yes," Notti heard herself stutter.
"Greetings your highness; your sister awaits you at the palace of Prince Tuthra.

His highness asked that I escort you safely through the village," he said proudly.

"Thank you," said Notti in her most regal manner and voice.

Not knowing what else to say, she worried knowing that she was neither a princess nor did she have a sister. Then she reminded herself that Grandpa Pine and Lady May Ya were looking out for her, and that she should just go along with it.

The soldier pulled the reins, and another soldier escorted her through the village. With a sigh of relief, Notti relaxed and decided to enjoy the sites. People watched the procession and suddenly Notti felt like a participant in a parade. She chuckled and wondered if she should wave to the people like a beauty queen. But because the soldiers looked so serious, she decided not to.

They rode through the main square and past a market where merchants sold fruits, grains, vegetables, and spices. On display were also fine cloths, beautiful garments, sandals, jewelry, ivory, and even small animals. Notti saw baboons and chickens in small cages, and goats tied up to stakes in the ground. Within the center of the square were several men arguing and frantically waving their arms. Notti wondered what they were upset about, and she suddenly recognized them as they rode closer.

"They're already here," she whispered, seeing BurK and the Kermas, and the rest of the captives who were untied and huddled together waiting to be sold. Notti's heart sank, and she wished she could do something to help. She held her breath hoping to pass by without notice, but suddenly she was spotted by YuBa. Yelling and waving his fists, he moved through the market toward her.

"Excuse me," said Notti to the soldier in her calmest and most polite voice. "May we please hurry? I really need to relieve myself," she grimaced.

"As you wish," replied the soldier to her left. With the twirl of his hand, he signaled to the other soldier to pick up the pace from a casual walk into an aggressive cantor. Notti leaned into Lightning and narrowly missed YuBa's grasp as he lunged at her. She turned back in time to see him stumble over his own feet and curse the ground with his fist.

BurK took advantage of the moment and grabbed the whip from a distracted Kerma. He whipped him repeatedly, sending him to the ground screaming and cursing in pain. Two more captives jumped on another trader, punching and knocking him out. The rest ran through the square and around merchants who tried to grab at them with no luck. Tables were knocked over, sending chickens and monkey cages flying everywhere. Notti turned one last time to see them running from the square and out of the village. Silently, she cheered them on as she steadily climbed the hill towards the palace entrance.

Notti held on tight to Lightning, as they rode by giant statues of nobility on thrones, luxurious gardens, and decorative ponds surrounded by flowers and palms.

Posted guards stood everywhere, and when the party came to a stop, one guard helped Notti down by graciously offering his hand.

"Thank you," said Notti as the guard nodded and led Lightning away. An escort soldier dismounted and motioned to Notti to follow him. They walked through a lush garden of exotic bloomed plants and flowers, and to a to a flight of stairs.

At the very top stood a boy who looked handsomely dressed in his gold tunic. He smiled with arms open and showing off his full cheeks and his deep-set dark eyes.

Across the room stood a bald robed man looking serious, and to his right stood Zinga. Notti could not contain herself, and up the stairs she flew with her arms open and ready to wrap herself around Zinga.

"Welcome, this is Prince Tuthra."

Notti's mouth dropped open, and she blinked rapidly trying to think of something regal to say.

"How do you do. I'm so glad to meet you," she managed to say. She felt amazed that a boy, not a man could be a prince. Notti noticed the robed man raise his eyebrows and look suspiciously at her while saying nothing.

Notti smiled at Zinga who also stood now with open and welcoming arms as Tuthra spoke.

"Welcome Notti, we are pleased you have arrived safely," he said with compassion.

"Let me introduce you to our high priest, War Ma," he said pointing to the robed man.

Notti could feel his glare piercing her skin like a sewing needle, as he looked at her soiled clothes. He bowed and Notti smiled, but she felt a sudden tightness in her stomach.

"Hello," said Notti with a smile to hide her discomfort.

"Greetings, and welcome to Dongo, said War Ma.

"In the morning shortly after sunrise, an order of seers will gather at the temple. They will pay tribute to the beginning of the fertile growing and harvest season. They do this so the river will rise and grace the land with nourishment. Please accept my invitation to attend," he said with an unusual glare.

"Sure thing," said Notti with a gentle nod.

"Thank you, War Ma, that will be all for now," interrupted Tuthra.

"We'll continue our discussion after the morning ceremony."

"Yes, very good," said War Ma as he departed down the stairs.

Tuthra continued his greeting and spoke up. "Zinga informed me to expect you to be tired and hungry. Please let our attendants' help you get refreshed before lunch," he said as he pointed to two young girls who giggled when they saw how filthy Notti looked.

"That sounds great," said Notti.

Zinga gave Notti a welcoming smile and her hand. Notti squeezed it and together they followed Tuthra and the two attendants into the palace. They walked down a great hall with colorfully painted depictions of people, half animal and half human sitting on thrones. Notti's heart fluttered with excitement knowing that this was a once in a lifetime experience. They came to a large copper door and Tuthra turned to the maidens and spoke gently.

"Take Notti to her room and attend to her needs. We shall expect her in the dining hall for some refreshment when she is ready."

The maidens nodded and opened the chamber doors.

"Thank you so much," said Notti. She turned to Zinga and tried to hold back her enthusiasm.

"Please come with me Zinga, I want to hear what you have been doing."

"Yes, of course. Please excuse me Tuthra," said Zinga with a slight nod.

Tuthra returned a nod of approval before leaving the hall through another entrance. Notti and Zinga followed the maidens into a spacious room.

A basin filled with water and floating white flowers greeted Notti, and she sighed knowing she would soon be clean. Looking around at the furniture and the unique and elaborate designs on the walls and floors, Notti felt delighted.

"This is the most elegant and beautiful bathroom I have ever been in," said Notti.

Zinga cleared her throat and looked at Notti sternly before seating herself upon a large cushion.

"Surely, you have bathrooms of equal beauty of your own?" replied a maiden.

"Why, yes, of course I do," said Notti.

"What I meant is that this bathroom is very special."

The maiden poured a cup of fragrant oil into the bath.

"Your bath is ready," she replied.

Notti slipped off her tunic and stepped into the stone basin tub.

"Oh, this feels great," she said as she slipped into its warmth.

With eyes closed, she leaned back, and her feet floated to the surface.

"Leave us now, please. I will call when she is finished," said Zinga.

The maidens bowed and left, and finally Notti and Zinga were alone.

"I can't believe I was going to be sold, and now I'm taking a bath," said Notti.

How did you know I was here, and when did you get here, and where is Wara?"

The questions came pouring out, until Zinga held up her hand signaling Notti to stop.   Notti did stop with her questions and instead replied.

"I'm sorry; it's just so hard to believe everything that I've been through since that night at the feast. I don't know what to ask first."

"Well," began Zinga.

"I was escorted here by two of Wara's attendants after you were captured. The others were sent to other villages with tasks.

Wara was told by Lady May Ya that you were on your way here, and I was told to ask Tuthra to send soldiers out to find you.

He is a good prince and does not believe in enslaving people, but his power is small because he our queen mother insists on purchasing slaves to build her sister a temple in the northern region.”

“Oh,” said Notti, while rubbing her skin free of dirt and grime with a large cloth sponge as Zinga continued.

“I told Tuthra we were separated during our journey, and he should have his soldiers look for you near the market.”

“Thank you, Zinga,” said Notti as she slipped deeper into the bath to wash her face and hair. When she finished, she sat back up and wrung out her now glistening hair. Zinga smiled, and with gratitude patted her beating heart, knowing that Notti was now safe.

“I still can’t believe what happened to me. To be captured and then rescued by Patrick” said Notti as she continued to vigorously use the sponge on her knees and feet.

“Please tell me about Tuthra and your family,” said Notti.

“Our father died in a battle seven years ago when Tuthra was only seven years old and I was four. An order of seers called the Mo’s, passed on the knowledge of the ancestors to Tuthra.”

“What kind of knowledge?” asked Notti.

“Ancient knowledge such as the dreamtime, and how to ask for guidance from the ancestors. And of course, how to use the crystal gems,” said Zinga before Notti asked another question.

“What happened to the seers?”

“Tuthra said that after their high seer mysteriously disappeared to a new land, that the other seers also began leaving and migrating to the new land. Before leaving they told our mother, Queen Ura, that they were going to a new home.

So, our mother summoned War Ma to take over the position of high seer.

in the new land across the sea the seers who left began a different practice and created their own order. They wished to return and influence our mother and our people away from ancestral belief and practice. and she should rule solely without ancestors or the spirit guides of nature".

"Wow, that must be really tough to have someone come in and try to change the way people think and practice their belief," said Notti as she reached for a towel.

"Yes, and now that Tuthra will soon be old enough to be the king, he admits that he needs help. He wants to uphold his father's ancestral legacy and practices. He doesn't want to be disrespectful to our mother, but he doesn't agree with this order for our people."

"That must also be hard," said Notti as she stepped out of the tub and wrapped the towel around herself.

"My mom is queen of our house, and what she says goes," continued Notti.

"Yes, well everyone is governed differently," said Zinga.

"Tuthra knows of a Mo seer in seclusion who would like to challenge the new order.

He has been patiently waiting for the right time to approach the head Mo seer.

"Wow, poor Tuthra. He must be really scared, and feel like he can't trust anyone," said Notti. She sat on a cushion to finish drying and put on a new tunic left by the maidans.

"I told Tuthra who you are and about the mission to find Lady Oshun of the river. Tonight, we leave to find the Mo seer. Notti, because you are here, you are welcome to come with us."

"Sure, I will if you think I can help."

"Yes, more help is better than less."
"Well, I guess we're not wasting any more time," said Notti.
"How old is your brother anyway?"
"He's fifteen."

"What about your mother, where is she?"

"She is in the north overseeing the construction of the temple. Tuthra expects her to return late tomorrow or the next day, and that is why we leave tonight"

They talked about the summit feast, and of course about Lady May Ya and Wara. Unaware that behind the thick drapes hid another maiden who heard every word of their conversation.

Zinga called in the maidens, who promptly brushed Notti's hair and rubbed her arms, legs, and face with fragrant oils. Upon her feet they laced up a pair of sandals, and around her neck they tied a beautiful gold necklace.

Notti ran her fingers over the necklace and smiled with sincere appreciation.

"The necklace is a present from Prince Tuthra said a maiden.

Notti thanked them both again as she and Zinga were led into the dining hall where Tuthra sat at the head of the table. Two male attendants patiently waited to serve them with bowls and platters of assorted raw and cooked food. Notti and Zinga were escorted and sat across from each other on handsomely crafted chairs. Notti thought back to the meals of dried bread and water she had eaten over the past days. Once again she sighed contently at the delicious sight.

"What a spread! Everything looks great," said Notti with enthusiasm at the sight of eating tasty food again. She was about to reach for a dish of figs and nuts when an attendant appeared and brought the plate to her.

"Thank you," said Notti as she took a generous helping.

Notti tried everything. There was roast duck, dates and grapes, pomegranate, and the same pudding she had at May Ya's feast. She ate with a ravenous appetite, and Tuthra amused himself by watching her, while he also conversed with Zinga.

He told her about the new temple his mother insisted on building for her older sister. How she had felt wronged about not being handed the position of queen. He further explained how he decided to agree to build her palace and temple as his way to keep peace between them.

Notti leaned back in the chair and rubbed her full belly.

"Wow, thanks for the great food," she said holding down a burp.

"You are welcome," said Tuthra. "Would you and Zinga like to take a walk through the gardens before I take my nap?"

"Sure," said Notti thinking, whoever heard of a fifteen-year-old taking a nap?

But suddenly she found herself yawning and thinking about a nap as well.

The walk through the gardens seemed long but pleasant, with so much to see and smell. There were large fig trees, beautiful and colorful flowers, and ponds covered with lily pads. They came out of the gardens and Notti noticed an old man sitting on a stool. He bowed and handed her and Zinga a small bouquet of lilies.

"The king is blessed to be in the company of such lovely young ladies," he said.

"Yes, indeed I am," responded Tuthra as he looked first at Zinga and then at Notti.

Notti lowered her head, not wanting her shyness to show. She never considered herself pretty or even lovely. She didn't even know what lovely looked like, but she was sure it was not her. She imagined herself as average, and figured the old man wanted to get on Tuthra's good side.

"Thank you," said both Notti and Zinga as they took the bouquets and made their way back to the temple gate.

Quite unexpectedly, Notti felt the soreness of her leg muscles from walking across the desert. and She felt more than ready for a nap.

Take them to their rooms so they may rest," Tuthra politely told a waiting maiden.

"Thank you so much for lunch and the walk," said Notti while holding down another yawn.

"You are welcome," replied Tuthra as the maiden escorted the girls into a bedroom.

"I hope you will be comfortable," said one maiden to Notti as she pulled back the bed covers. "Let me help you with your shoes and jewelry."

Notti sat on the edge of the bed and the maiden unlaced Notti's sandals. She was about to lift off the band over her bracelet, when Notti said, "Oh no, I'll just leave my jewelry on."

When they were both tucked in, Zinga waved the maiden away, letting her know she was fine and dd not need any more attention. "As you wish," said the maiden respectfully, and she left.

Notti's head hit the pillow, and in a minute, she fell asleep and into her dreams. She dreamt she was running in slow motion through the desert. Her legs were growing heavy with every step. She heard galloping from behind. When she turned, a woman on horseback galloped towards her. She wore a crown, and her hair flared wildly in the wind. Notti tried to run faster. The woman yelled and shook her fist, saying, "return the bracelet or die!" Fearful, Notti stumble eeing the river, and dove in to escape the threat of an angry woman.

Chapter Twenty-One

PO

"Wake up Notti, we're leaving now, so wake up," whispered Zinga.

Notti opened her eyes and immediately felt for her bracelet. With a sigh of relief, she sat up to see Zinga standing beside her bed holding a large lit candle.

"Just once, I would like to wake up normally and peacefully without a lightning bolt, or a threatening slave trader, or in the middle of the night," said Notti with a long yawn.

"How did it get dark so fast?"

"You've been asleep for a long while, and I would have awakened you sooner, but Tuthra said to let you sleep after your terrible ordeal with the traders."

"That's great, thanks. I haven't slept on a real bed since I left home."

Notti reluctantly slid out of bed, tied up her sandals, and was soon following Zinga down the palace corridor. Quietly they tiptoed out into the stables.

"Good evening, Notti and Zinga," said Tuthra, while holding the reins of Lightning and two other horses. "I trust you slept well Notti?"

"Well, yes," said Notti, thinking of the crazy woman in her dream.

"Good," he said helping each onto saddles.

"To avoid suspicion, I've alerted my personal servant to let him know that we will be watching the star constellations by the river."

Tuthra explained to Notti and Zinga his plan for them to head south along the river, and then east to the outskirts of the village. There, they would look for the cave where the old seer lived hiding. He shared how his father, shortly before his death, took him to meet the old man. Tuthra had agreed to keep a vow of secrecy about his whereabouts. He was now going to break that vow because he knew he had to.

He mounted his own horse, and off they rode out of the temple grounds and towards the Oshun River. In the distance the temple glowed in the moon-lit sky. Tuthra slowed his horse to a walk and took a long look back. Notti fumbled with her reins, but Lightning already sensed the change and slowed his pace to walk with the others. Surrounded by a star-filled sky, lay the village that appeared loud and busy during the day. Now it slept peacefully in the quiet of the night. Notti and Zinga gazed as Tuthra spoke.

"We must help Dongo. For in her wake is an evil that is running through her like a disease gone rampant in a man's blood. Somehow, we must help the people see the sacredness of this land and honor all the gifts with which we have. If they choose to worship gold and power, then I will be sad by what I see. I refuse to watch all my father's good work be buried with him."

Tuthra turned away, and the three rode on now with purpose and with haste.

Before long they turned west to a small valley by the river. Tuthra slowed the pace. Notti watched him look from side to side as they entered a grove of palms. She wondered what he could be looking for. She hoped he hadn't lost something important.

Tuthra stopped just as they heard a small rustle from behind a large palm tree. Out jumped the smallest man Notti had ever seen, holding a bull's horn. He stood no taller than an eight-year-old child while wearing nothing but a white loin cloth.

Tuthra recognized him at once and reached down to pull him up on to his horse. The little man gave Tuthra a friendly pat on his shoulders.

"This is Po, keeper of the tunnel," announced Tuthra.

Notti and Zinga nodded a greeting. Po put the horn to his lips and blew a low and steady tone. Two other small men jumped out from behind a boulder and ran over to two large boulders. They placed their palms on each side of it. With little effort, they rolled the boulders away from the cave entrance.

"Wait," whispered Tuthra. "Listen, someone is coming."

Po scrambled up the tree. He looked toward the coming sound. Notti suddenly felt her stomach tighten and her heartbeat accelerated. Po held up four fingers and nodded.

"It's four horses; someone has followed us. Quickly, into the cave. Everyone dismounted, and Po took the reins of all three horses and tied them each to a stake. He grabbed one of two lit torches on the wall then proceeded through the tunnel.

Notti was about to say something when Tuthra put a finger to his lips. He could hear faint voices and horses stomping.

"They must be here somewhere," they heard someone say.

"Spread out and look for their tracks."

Tuthra looked puzzled, but he motioned to Notti and Zinga to follow Po. He instead waited and listened. Through the dimly lit cave they trekked, watching their shadows against the walls, and feeling the tension of the unknown.

"Wow," whispered Notti.

Her word bounced and echoed back to her, as she moved closer to Zinga and lowered her head before speaking.

"A seer who lives in a cave, what a strange thing," she continued.

"While you rested," began Zinga.

"Tuthra shared with me the seer's story. He lives here because of his unique gifts and visions. Before he went into hiding, he was known as a master healer. Many sought his council and guidance. However, when new seers migrated and settled in

Dongo, they disagreed with the knowledge and teachings of the masters. They recruited most of the younger seers and gave them false promises about continuing their practice. When the older Mo seer died, Master Shu was the only seer left. When the seers found this out, they sent a messenger to silence him if he did not stop sharing his wisdom."

"Do the seers know that Master Shu is still alive?" asked Notti.

"Yes, because each time a master dies, the male lion, who is a sacred messenger to his order, appears at the entrance to their temple and roars three times. There has been no lion since his disappearance," said Zinga.

"How scary, what does the lion do after he roars?"
"The lion will stay until another is chosen to take the masters' place," said Zinga.
"What does the master of an order do?" asked Notti.
"Master Shu is a direct descendant of Shu Wa, the lord of mortal knowledge and education," continued Zinga.
"Wow that sounds important," whispered Notti with her raised eyebrows.
"Tuthra says the knowledge is passed on from each generation of master's to the chiefs and kings, so they may be a guide for their people," replied Zinga.

"What about places that don't have a chief or like in Wara's village?" asked Notti.

"That is where the elders of the family play an important role. They pass on the knowledge in the present or once they've departed," replied Zinga.

"Oh, like my grandfather," said Notti just as Tuthra caught up to them. Zinga nodded before turning her attention to Tuthra.

"Who is it, were you able to tell?" persisted Zinga. "

No," said Tuthra out of breath. "But whoever it is will continue to look for us, so we must find another way out," he said coldly.

Notti could see he was angry with himself for being followed, but Po led them to a deep opening and into another cavern. A gentle light flooded through the opening, and Po played a soft tune with his horn. The song struck a chord in Notti's memory, and she wondered why it sounded so familiar.

Tuthra thanked Po and asked him to check on the horses and the entrance. Po nodded then hurried past them with a look of urgency.

Carefully, they took turns stepping into the narrow opening. Notti found she had to bend down to guide herself through it successfully. Once inside she was able to stand. In the center of the cavern, lay a large tranquil pool. In one of the corners lay a flat stone surrounded by grass woven cushions next to oil burning bowls.

"Come, we must sit," whispered Tuthra. They each sat on a cushion near the pool.

"What you are about to see and hear is known only to me and a few caretakers like Po," said Tuthra in a serious tone. Notti and Zinga understood and nodded respectfully.

"Your secret is safe with us, and we thank you for having the courage to share it with us," said Zinga. The three sat in silence to wait and ponder what would come.

Chapter Twenty-Two

MASTER SHU

They must have been sitting for some time because Notti's crossed legs went numb, and her head nodded in and out of sleep several times. The sound of a giant gulp popped her head out of temporary slumber. They all let out a small gasp as a fountain of water burst from the center of the pool. The water shot straight up to the ceiling, and Notti fell back off her cushion. Zinga grabbed her hand to help her back up. Together they watched the fountain part and unfold like the petals of a blooming flower.

From the center emerged first a head, followed by a pair of broad shoulders. An enchanting older man with long white hair and a long white beard. And finally, a long fish tail with scales of turquoise and green iridescent hues rose to the ceiling. Stars danced in his eyes from the reflective light. His smile bore sweetness and a love which comes only from the kindest and most generous of hearts. Around his neck hung an ivory shaped diamond pendent. On his wrist, he wore a golden bracelet adorned with many crystal gems.

"Greeting, Master Shu. We have traveled a great distance and are grateful and ready to receive your words," said Tuthra as he respectively nodded his head.

"It is an honor dear Tuthra," said Master Shu as he stood balanced on the tip of his tail.

"Please bring me my robe and my stone seat so I may sit and converse with you for a while. Remember first to ask the stone permission to be moved, and if it agrees, it will allow you to carry it without its weight."

Tuthra did as he was asked, by first grabbing and handing him his robe, and then asking the rock if it would accept being moved. Tuthra waited only a minute and then lifted the stone with minimal effort. Notti and Zinga watched with amazement as Tuthra set down the large stone. Master Shu quickly put on his robe, then sat on the rock, and swung his tail over to rest on the small rocks around the pond. He proceeded to wring out the water from his hair and beard, before giving his guests his sincere and full attention.

"How may I be of assistance to all of you?"

Tuthra spoke up again.

"My sister and friend arrived at my temple from a gathering. There they were gifted with the dreamtime gems from Lady May Ya. We come to you in hopes of receiving your guidance in the matter of Lady Oshun's disappearance, and how we may help to find her. You know my father was a good king. And that he tried to lead his people back to the ways of our humble and giving ancestors. Just before his death he confided in me. He said his reign had been difficult with much opposition and small gains."

"Yes, I am aware of this unfortunate truth, for I knew you father's dilemma well," said Shu in the gentlest of voice. He stroked his hair and sighed while reflecting on Tuthra's words. He turned to look deeply into the pool and then passed his hand over the surface.

He motioned to the children to join him by his side. As he spoke, the pool began to swirl, changing from emerald, green to black. Tuthra and the girls scooted up alongside of Shu in time to see an image of a man suddenly appear. Master Shu looked at each of them before speaking.

"Of course, our life does not always follow the exact course we first envisioned it to become," he said with now a deep and resonating voice.

"As with your father and his father before him, they envisioned a civilization founded on the principles of love, unity and the dreamtime world."

"Oh yes, my great-grandfather," cried Tuthra.

Master Shu nodded saying, "yes Tuthra he was King Menes. Now listen to his message."

Notti sat up a little straighter and looked with awe into the pool.

"This is the first secret of the ancestors," said King Menes.

"The dream world is here with us, and willing to respond to our call if the intention is good and from love. Tuthra, you are now the light who leads the way for the people of the Oshun Valley. Our visions will now be yours, and it is time for you to learn the secrets of the ancestors as you search for truth."

King Menes then looked at Zinga and Notti as he continued his message.

"In each of you resides the knowledge of a life before you were born into the physical life you have now. Learning how to release knowledge from your heart so you may help humanity is your greatest task.

Please strive from within, for love and unity has great power. Those who are trapped in fear will influence others and spread their manner often knowing that they do. Such is the way of much of the world. This way must change. Be willing to be a part of this change. Listen and learn well, and you will succeed in making a difference."

With his final words, King Menes faded back into the darkness of the pool. Master Shu passed his hand over the pool, and it returned to its emerald, green color.

He looked at the children and sighed heavily.

"We have not been able to communicate with Lady Oshun. With her absence there is no out pouring of her affections to make the river fertile. As a result, the crops are failing, and food is becoming scarce."

"Yes," said Tuthra. "I have seen the desperation in the villagers, and with the merchants in the marketplace, but where can Lady Oshun be?"

"I don't know, but I do believe the new order of seers is behind her disappearance, for they are proclaiming that the villager's lords and ladies have abandoned the people," said

Master Shu. Sadness overcame him as the sparkles in his eyes suddenly disappeared.

"How cruel," said Notti, while thinking of how confident she felt knowing that Grandpa Pine was watching over her.

"Yes, it is terribly cruel, and we must find a way to stop the lies," said Shu.

"Where is this new order and who is their master? I will seek them out and send them back to where they came from," commanded Tuthra.

Suddenly, the urgent sound of a horn could be heard from the corridor. Tuthra stood and grabbed his dagger.

"They have found a way in. Master Shu, we have been followed," said Tuthra in a panic.

Shu had already disappeared into the pool, leaving a large ripple spreading to the outer rim.

"Master Shu, Master Shu," called Tuthra as he leaned over the pool desperately searching for him. They heard voices approaching, and Notti and Zinga rushed to stand beside Tuthra.

"What should we do, and who's after us?" pleaded Notti with her racing heart.

The fear of capture by the traders seized her with memories of her recent entrapment. They heard another gulp, and together they stepped back as a surge of water from the pool rose to the ceiling. Up popped Shu, and beside him emerged a young woman.

"Hurry," said Shu, lifting himself from the water and swinging his tail around to rest on the flat stone.

"This is my daughter Shu Ra, and she will take you through the pool and into the river. Close to here is an underwater entrance into the tomb of your father. From there you can find your way back to the main entrance and eventually back to your village. I am sorry I could not help you more, but I will stay here and wait for the intruders."

Daughter Shu Ra rose from the pool to the tip of her tail and bowed out of respect to Tuthra and his guests.

"I am at your service," she said respectfully in her squeaky voice, which Notti thought sounded like a mouse.

She wondered if Shu Ra was teased as a little girl by other children.

"No Master Shu, I will not leave you; let me stay instead," said Tuthra, holding up his knife. Master Shu bowed with humility and shook his head.

"No, you and your friends must find and help Lady Oshun. Into the pool you must now go," he said turning to Zinga and Notti.

"You want us to go down into the pool and swim all the way to a tomb?" asked Notti nervously. "Can we do this on one breath?"

"Oh, how ignorant of me to assume you know how. You must use your bracelets. Take the purple gem and envision yourself breathing underwater. Believe that you can, and you will," said Shu while reaching for Tuthra's wrist and slipping the bracelet on him.

"This sacred bracelet of the ancestors is from your father, and I have held it since he entrusted it to me," said Shu.

Tuthra looked into Shu's eyes with gratitude.

"You will have to wait until we meet again for your lessons on the rest of the gems," said Shu, as his legs split apart, and his webbed feet separated into toes.

Notti could not believe her eyes and wondered how a tail could become legs.

"Hurry Notti, they're coming," whispered Zinga.

Notti scrambled to retrieve her pouch just as the strange and haunting voices sounded closer. Finding the purple gem, she placed it in the bevel and magically it sealed in tightly.

"They're here," said Tuthra with a look of dismay. Po stumbled through the entrance with a whip wrapped around his neck. A large foot pushed Po down to his knees, and he cried out in despair.

"He's bleeding," whispered Notti with a need to run and help.

Tuthra and Zinga backed up to the edge of the pool and tugged at Notti to conceal Shu Ra.

"Be ready to jump," whispered Tuthra as he grabbed each of their arms. They all envisioned with clarity of mind, breathing under the water.

"Well, well, who do we have here? It looks as if we have arrived just in time," said a voice.

Stepping into the cavern, War Ma grinned with his hand firmly holding the whip. Tuthra gritted his teeth in disgust just as another figure clothed in a white robe emerged with a bowed head. He stood erect, and with a graceful hand pulled back the hood to let it fall around its shoulders.

"Hello, my son," said Tuthra's mother. "What an unpleasant surprise to see you with the man responsible for your father's death. Nana overheard your plans, and we followed to seek revenge on this traitor. With Master Shu's guidance from the ancestors, he advised your father to strike a battle with the kingdom of Mu Land".

"Mother!" gasped Tuthra as he staggered back in shock. But it was all he could say, for he fell back in horror clutching Zinga and Notti in his grip and taking them down with him into the emerald pool.

Chapter Twenty-Three

LADY OSHUN

Notti fell into the cool green water with barely enough time to catch and hold her breath. With the weight of her clothes, she sank quickly, and when she looked up, there were two figures leaning over the pool watching their descent. Notti moved freely but held her breath tightly until she felt as if her lungs would burst.

"I'm afraid I can't," thought Notti.
"You must," said a voice sounding like Tuthra. Notti turned around to see Tuthra nodding.
"Breathe Notti, breathe. We can speak to each other through our thoughts."

"Yes," said Zinga. *"Just believe, and you will breathe!"*

Notti could not hold it in any longer and let go of her breath. She felt water rush into her mouth and nostrils, before flooding into her lungs. Tightening up, she expected to gag, but the cool flow of water through her was all she could feel.

"I don't know how, but I'm breathing," Notti thought with delight.

Shu Ra waved her arms for everyone's attention. Notti gracefully treaded water by swaying her legs. She could not imagine what Tuthra must be feeling about seeing his mother and his personal aide.

"He must be very brave," thought Notti.

"Thank you, Notti," thought Tuthra. *"I am utterly confused."*

"Do not worry," thought Shu Ra in her mousey voice.

"My father will take care of the situation. Everyone, I will take you now to the tomb. Be prepared, for along with the breath of water comes the joining of your legs and the webbing of your feet. This will last only as long as you remain under the water, so do not despair that you have lost your legs forever. Your eyes will take in all light, and this will allow you to see a good distance in front of you. Just be careful not to swim too fast or too far ahead of everyone else".

Shu Ra's words faded out of Notti's mind, as she was still overwhelmed with her new gift of underwater breathing. A warm sensation suddenly came over her thighs and calves, and she felt them pulling together while her toes stretched and spread apart for a webbed tissue to form between them.

"I'm turning into a fish," thought Notti.

"Relax Notti, and don't resist the transformation," said Shu Ra, as she swam ahead to show them all how to use their new tails.

Notti looked down at her legs, joined together and covered with scales. She could feel the scales popping out of her skin and traveling over her knees, up her thighs, and under her tunic. Shaking off her disbelief, she tried moving her tail back and forth and found that it was easy. Now she needed to know how to move in a direction. She watched Shu Ra's movements and tried again. Tuthra and Zinga were also watching and practicing, and soon they were all swimming masterfully within the pool.

"Stay close to me, everyone. We will swim through a small channel, and then we will meet the current of Oshun. Depending on the moon, we will not know the strength of the water until we reach its mouth," thought Shu Ra.   *"To enter this domain, you must do so with honor or pay with your life!"*

"What? What are you talking about?" asked Notti.
"Who, me?" thought Zinga.
"No, this rock creature is talking to me," said Notti.
"What rock creature?" asked Tuthra?

Notti turned to point to the creature, but when she turned back the creature had vanished.

"It was there," thought Notti, as they swam towards the channel.

"Do not trouble yourself Notti with what you imagined; you are approaching the realm of Lady Oshun."

Notti could feel the power of the water pushing her back, so she whipped her tail back and forth forcibly.

"You will have to swim a little harder to get through, but it will be brief," thought Shu Ra.

Indeed, it was just as she said, because the water rushed and churned through the narrow passage. The small group pulled together and swam harder with their tails cutting through the water like canoe paddles. Notti looked ahead and saw piercing rays of brown and yellow across their path. It was the energy of the river Oshun. In a minute, they were all swept up by the power of her current and magnificence.

Notti felt so taken in by it all. But once the water had calmed, she swam on her back and gazed up at the moon's reflection resting over the surface. She dove deep to feel the rush of warm water against her skin. Finally, she spun around slowly just like the last seconds of a spinning top before it rests on its side.

"Notti, this way!" thought Zinga.

Notti awoke from her daydreaming and looked for the others. The water was now sparse and lifeless, and a sudden discomfort came over her.

"Watch out," she heard Shu Ra shout.
"It is too late, we're trapped," came Tuthra's voice.
"Everyone, try not to struggle as it will only get worse," thought Shu Ra.

Notti's heart pounded and she swam faster towards their thoughts. The water quickly turned murky, and it was difficult to see. She swam a little further, and there in the distance, she saw each one suspended in an awkward position.

"Notti stay back! Do not come any closer," thought Tuthra.

Notti pulled back with her tail and slowed herself down. Her friends hung tangled in a large net with several large fish.

"What should I do? I've got to get you out of there," thought Notti as she frantically swam around them.

"My dagger is too small to cut through these ropes. You will have to get help," thought Tuthra.
"Help from where?" panicked Notti.

"Go to the tomb. There will be guards there. Ask them to help," thought Shu Ra.

"How do I get there? I don't know where to go!"

"Swim past us until you get to a bend in the river," thought Shu Ra with urgency.

"Look to your right for a pile of six large stones. The stones are shaped like a crocodile and that is the entrance to the tomb. Go into the corridor where you will see guards posted. Hurry, before the fishermen return to check their nets, and before we are discovered by the crocodiles."

Notti swam as fast as she could, repeating the instructions over and over in her mind. Swimming deeper led her to clearer water, so she dove into the river's depths.

"My friends are in trouble, and I'm swimming in the river. This is so crazy! If I ever get home, nobody's going to believe me."

She thought of Patrick and Hanna, and even of her teacher Mr. Johnson, who now all seemed so far away. Something brushed against her and startled her. When she looked there was nothing. She thought about how the crates and ropes had turned into a lion and snakes on the pirate ship. She wondered if the same could happen in the river. Notti watched carefully, making sure she did not bump into anything that might become something.

"I've been swimming for a while. Maybe I missed the entrance," she thought hoping Shu Ra would hear her and answer. With no response, her fears grew.

"I must have missed it! No, there's the bend, I'm almost there," she thought with relief.

Notti watched the rocks and saw several piles, but nothing resembling a crocodile. Uncertain, she swam on when suddenly a voice rang out, *"Stop!"*

Abruptly, Notti did as she was told, while she looked for the voice. And just as Shu Ra had said, there piled next to a cluster of river weeds sat an unusually shaped pile of rocks. Notti let out a small gasp, when suddenly the rock pile took on the appearance of a crocodile.

It stood on two hind legs with a typical crocodile grin. Though it did not move, it appeared to be real. Notti swam past the crocodile rocks with caution. Fortunately, it continued to stand erect, pointed its elongated nose toward the entrance with its bulging eyes. The further Notti swam, the shallower the water became. Soon she came up to the surface and took her first breath. Water poured from her nose and mouth as the air pushed its way in. She coughed a little, but that was all. She effortlessly breathed in the air.

Notti looked around and saw that she was in a narrow canal within another tunneled cavern. Suddenly, a pair of eyes peered at her from holes and crevices in the rock wall. Her stomach tightened and her heart raced. She felt her every move would be watched. A guard sitting on a flat rock saw Notti and immediately aimed his spear at her. Notti froze, not saying a word. She thought back to her encounter with the painted men with their spears and wondered if he would attack. The guard said nothing but directed her to swim toward a man seated on the top of a stone step. He stood and glared down at Notti.

"Who are you and on what authority do you have to enter this tomb?"

"My name is Notti, and my friends are in trouble. They sent me here to ask for help," said Notti. Her stomach continued to tighten, and the peering eyes continued to watch.

"Who said you could ask for help?"

"Master Shu's daughter, Shu Ra sent me here. Please hurry before it's too late."

The glaring eyed guard called for another guard who appeared from behind a jagged wall.

"Tell his Excellency's advisor that a child sent by Shu Ra seeks immediate help."

The guard nodded and disappeared behind the rock wall. He appeared again seconds later followed by a hobbling and disfigured old woman. She startled Notti, but her gentle smile eased Notti's first impression, and for a moment she relaxed.

"Yes child, what brings you to the late king's tomb?" the woman asked curiously.

"I need your help. Shu Ra sent me, and she and my friends are trapped in a fisherman's net."

"Where?" asked the advisor as she raised her eyebrows with interest.

"They're in the river near Master Shu's Pond.

"Are they dead?" she asked with a strange smirk.

"Oh! Well, I hope they are not. They were alive when I left them," answered Notti.

"And where is this Master Shu?"

"He's been captured by Prince Tuthra's mother. We escaped through the emerald pool. Won't you please hurry? They're in a fisherman's net and they're in danger."

"Quickly," said the old woman to the glaring guard.

"Gather up three men and take them to where the child speaks of. Use your swords of light, for the nets will be of a heavy rope."

The guards all bowed and dove into the water then raced through the corridor.

"Wait for me," cried Notti, but she was stopped by the old woman's voice.

"No! Stay here, for you will not be able to keep up with them. They travel at the speed of light and will swim with the current. Come and tell me about yourself while we wait. Do not be afraid; your friends will be brought here soon enough. Now come up on the rocks and rest from your long swim. I have some fruit to refresh you."

Notti pulled herself out of the water and threw her tail onto a flat rock with a thud. She felt the warm sensation return to her thighs and calves. She watched in amazement as her legs separated, and her web feet shrank back into her toes. Notti shook her head in continued wonder and awe. She wrung out her dripping tunic and followed the old woman to behind the rock wal

With her grossly wrinkled and bulging veined hand, the woman gave Notti a large towel. Notti gratefully wrapped it around her shoulders like a shawl.

"Are you really an advisor?" asked Notti.

"Yes, I am, and I reside in this tomb to oversee any requests the late king may have while waiting for his judgment in the underworld. Sit down child and tell me what you will," she concluded softly.

Notti wanted to ask what she meant by judgment. However, she was so taken back by the old woman's brown decayed teeth and gray straggly hair clumps that she could not find the words. Notti looked into her dark glossy eyes and grimaced at the red lines running across her pupils. Leaning back, Notti noticed how the woman's back was hunched over and wondered if she was a witch. She swallowed hard and finally mustered up the courage to say something.

"Well, there's not much to tell except that my friends and I are trying to find out what happened to Lady Oshun. Master Shu told us that not too long-ago people were peaceful and honored their friends and neighbors. Now they're always at war and enslaving people to do their work for them. He told us that the people used to honor Lady Oshun for taking care of them, but now she's disappeared, and the land is dying," said Notti with deep empathy.

The old woman listened closely and would occasionally nod as if she understood, So Notti continued.

"We thought Master Shu would help us find Lady Oshun, but he's probably locked up in a prison by now."

"He told you this, did he? Well, I would have to say Master Shu is a very mistaken man. The people do not honor Lady Oshun," she said raising her voice.

"They honor only gold; and who has the gold? The kings and queens of other lands have it. They would just as soon sell their brother for a bag of gold. There is no honor. It is lost and forgotten, because all the people want from Lady Oshun is river water!" The old woman was shouting now.

"Water is needed for their homes, crops, and to catch fish. She cannot take care of people with no honor! They neither ask for protection nor for guidance. They never bring offerings nor give thanks and praises," she defiantly finished.

Notti shifted uncomfortably on the rock before clearing her throat to speak.

"Why would Master Shu tell PrinceTuthra to find Lady Oshun, if the people don't honor her?"

"Hmm, is Prince Tuthra one of your friends trapped in the nets?"
"Yes, he is," said Notti.

"Well, I do not know why Master Shu sent you, a child. Perhaps he spoke in haste because he feared your capture. It is most interesting though."

She smiled while handing Notti a small plate of fruit. When Notti reached for the plate, her sleeve pulled back revealing her bracelet, which sent the old hag's eyebrows shooting up.

"Here you are child, now eat."

Notti was not particularly hungry after her large meal at King Tuthra's temple. But not wanting to offend the old woman she took a piece of pineapple and a fig.

"Where am I anyway?" asked Notti before taking a bite.
"You are beneath the temple," she said not taking her eyes from Notti's silver bracelet.
"Do you mean the temple is right over us?"
"Yes, indeed it is my child."
"Wow, that's amazing," said Notti taking a bite of the fig with a grim face at the taste.

"I am sorry. The fruit must not be quite ripe yet," said the hag with a strange grin.

Notti heard voices and turned towards the canal. "They're here!"

She stood but fell back against the rock.

"I guess I'm not used to having my legs back," she said standing up again. But it was more than her legs because she felt a sudden wave of dizziness. She reached for the wall for support.

"Notti, Notti, where are you?" she heard Tuthra call.

"I'm right here," she answered back as she staggered out from behind the wall toward the canal. Tuthra and Zinga floated in the water with the guards by their sides, but unexpectedly they faded in and out of Notti's focus.

"I don't feel so well," she whispered as she tripped over a stone and fell, hitting the floor with a somber thud into unconsciousness.

"Notti, what is the matter?" screamed Zinga. The old woman emerged like a shadow from behind the wall. She smiled as she stepped over Notti.

"This is a fortunate day to have Prince Tuthra, and his two companions delivered to me. And what of daughter Shu Ra, where is she?"

"Dead," shouted Tuthra. "She was slain by your butcher without mercy."

"She tried to get away," spoke up a guard in defense as he held tight to them both.

"No matter, as she is of no use to me alive. It is these who concern me now. What are we to do with Lady Oshun's people, especially a prince who has ceased to honor me? Am I to have no respect? I think not! We will put an end to it right now. What do you say little prince? Choose your death, and then you will bow to me."

"Who are you, and where is Lady Oshun, the giver of life to the land and its people? What has happened to Notti?" shouted Tuthra.

"Ha, ha, ha," the hag crackled while throwing her head back.

"This withered body is not who I am," she shouted, as her body shed its wrinkled skin.

Tuthra and Zinga gasped and tried to swim back, but once again the guards held firm. The hag's gray hair fell to the ground and black waves of wool as dark as a moonless night sprouted from her scalp. The creature's face blistered like hot lava as it took on the form of a handsome male. He stood in a magnificent form and stately in height. Almond eyes filled his sockets with eternal dark pools emitting a brilliant light. His full lips parted, revealing rows of glistening pearl white teeth. The rocks cried, laughed, and screamed as the being grew from its aging shell to double in size. Reaching the cavern ceiling, it sat and stretched out its large muscular arms and with a clenched fist as he bellowed.

"Oshun is slave to me, for I am Lord Seb of the Underworld."

Chapter Twenty-Four

LORD SEB

"Take them all to the fire pit," roared Seb.

"I will return at daybreak to decide the fate of three more slaves for my paradise. And when I pass judgment, I will grant you all into my army. Bring the daughter of Shu as well and put her in the shadow-filled pits below. Take the prince and the other below and drag this sleeping one with you. The tonic will wear off soon," he commanded as he kicked Notti over.

A guard with a sullen expression lurched through the water to climb up onto the shore. As his feet and toes returned, he grabbed Notti and threw her over his shoulder like a sack of potatoes before waiting for his next order.

"Wait," called Seb. "Put her in my chambers. This one has more to tell me."

"What have you done to Notti, you demon?" screamed Zinga.

The guards dragged Tuthra and Zinga through the canal.

"Lady Oshun will not look kindly on this," echoed Zinga's voice.

"How dare Lady Oshun interfere with me, she has no power here. Oshun is mine and so are her people," he said licking his lips with a delicious smile.

"Open," he uttered, placing his hands upon two immense boulders.

Obediently the boulders pulled apart, and Seb entered a steaming stench before the enormous rocks sealed shut behind him.

With Notti draped over the guard shoulder, he bumbled through another corridor and up into Seb's chamber. Briefly his eyes scanned past a small throne, a large woven hammock, and a flat rock resembling an altar, before spotting a small cot under a lit torch.

"I do not envy you little girl," he said throwing her down on the cot.

For a moment he gazed at her innocence and wondered what her fate would be.

"He wasn't always a monster," whispered the guard, as he closed the rock door and stood by it.

Zinga and Tuthra were forced into a smaller cavern with a gated exit blocking a pool of crocodiles. The other guard roped them both to a post on a sandy floor and bolted the door.

Groaning, they waited and watched their legs and toes return before helping one another up.

"I blame myself for this entrapment," cried Tuthra.

He buried his face into his hands and trembled uncontrollably.

"My mother has been plotting against me and what am I to do?"

Zinga leaned to his side to give him comfort and assurance.

"Oh no Tuthra, how could you have known?"

Zinga patted his back and tried to give him reassurance. Tuthra shook his head, and she could feel the tension mounting on his shoulders.

"We must think of a way out of here," cried Zinga.

"Yes! Thank you for understanding and forgive me for such a childish display. We will find a way out, and we will find Notti," whispered Tuthra.

They were dripping wet, and the air chilled them to the bone. Zinga shivered and Tuthra put his arms around her and pulled her close. They sank down onto the cold ground and leaned against a rock wall. Zinga rested her head on Tuthra's shoulder and reached for her bag of gems.

"I will try to contact Lady May Ya even if the lord thinks she is powerless here," said Zinga.

Tuthra nodded and squeezed her arm. Zinga placed a finger on the green gem and closed her eyes to collect her thoughts and visualize Lady May Ya.

"Lady May Ya," she whispered. "We ask for your help and guidance. On our way to find Lady Oshun we were captured by Lord Seb. We are trapped behind the walls of a tomb. Lord Seb will return at dawn to decide our fate. Hear me and please come to our aide."

Zinga repeated her prayer over and over again until her eyes slowly closed, and she fell asleep.

Tuthra watched her fall asleep in his arms, and not until that moment did, he realize her beauty. Her wet hair fell upon her face, and he gently brushed it aside, wishing he had never brought her nor Notti into Master Shu's cavern. Through the gate he could see shadowy figures swimming back and forth and looking for a way in. Would their fate be food for the crocodiles? Wearily, he looked at the latch on the gate and wondered.

"There must be a way out of here. There must be a way," he repeated.

The weight of their dilemma brought his head down and his eyes also closed once, then twice, before he too fell asleep.

Her dream was of Wara smiling and pointing to her. Notti placed her hand over her own heart and slowly said Notti. Wara repeated her name and they both nodded and sighed. Wara gently took her hand and led her to a cot.

"Thank you Wara for your kindness. I will never forget you. And when I get home, I will tell Grandpa Pine and my new friends my dreamtime story, and about you too."

Chapter Twenty-Five

PITS OF THE DEAD

Notti slept on the canvas cot, unaware of a lavender fragrant mist drifting through the corridor. It drifted past the sleeping guard and traveled under the sealed gate. The mist floated across the ground and spread quickly over Notti until it covered her completely. Suddenly, from it came a gentle and hushed voice.

"Awaken dear Notti. Rise from your unconscious and hear my call. Lady Oshun is dying in the hands of Lord Seb. Arise and release her from bondage."

Notti slowly opened her eyes but then squeezed them shut as a shooting pain exploded from her forehead. A menacing odor filled her nostrils, and she coughed before rolling over on to her side. Blinking rapidly, she let her eyes adjust to the darkness, and again she felt a shooting pain. She touched her head to check for any blood but found instead a large swollen bump.

"Where am I?" she whispered.

Gently, she rubbed the bump in hopes of making the pain go away. Inching off the cot, she searched for the door, but found none, and not even a window.

"Is this a tomb? I can't remember how I got here," she said as a stench filled her nostrils.

"Augh, what stinks? It smells like rotten eggs."

Standing up, she followed the smell until it led to a wall behind her. Running her hand across the stone wall, she felt heat coming in between the cracks. She wondered if there was a hidden passage. So, pressing on each stone, she expected one of them to budge, but not one did. Remembering what Master Shu had shown her, she firmly placed her hands on the wall and closed her eyes as she spoke to the stones.

"Stone wall," she whispered, "would you kindly allow me to move some of you so I may get out of this room?"

Notti pressed again on each stone, and just as she was having doubts in her attempts, one of the stones moved. She pushed a little harder and it rolled away to reveal a small opening. Three more stones allowed her to roll them aside and to create a large enough opening for her to squeeze through.

The odor engulfed her sinuses, but she quickly pinched her nose close. Looking inside she could see a lit torch pocketed and on the wall. Not knowing what might be ahead, Notti crawled until she reached a balcony. Pulling herself up, she peered over the railing and was struck with horror at the sight of a creature. Notti sat down with a quiet thud and put her hand over her mouth to keep from gasping out loud.

"It's a creature, but I will be okay," she told herself in a nervous whisper.

Her heart pounded so loudly that she feared the creature might hear her. She knew she had to find her friends, so once again she pulled herself up and peered over the railing. The ground supported one pit after another, and in each were the shadows of people.

As many as a hundred men, women, and children stood motionless. The creature sat on a crude stone throne, while holding a scepter and wearing a metal crown.

"What right has Oshun to meddle into my affairs?" she heard the creature say.

"Does she not know the pain I have suffered from being ignored?"

He looked at a small, roofed cage in the corner of the room and continued.

"You honor me now, don't you Oshun?"
Notti's eyes widened as she listened and watched him turn toward all the people.
"Am I not your lord, and not Oshun and her dreamtime gems, but me Seb Lord of the underworld?"
When there was no answer, he sighed and spoke out again.
"I am also your lord, am I not Oshun?"

"*It's Lady Oshun,*" thought Notti with both excitement and fear as she remained hidden.

"You are my prisoner, and you will do as I command," continued Lord Seb.

"Not until I surrender," said Lady Oshun with a louder and confident voice.

"Even then you will not be lord to me, but only now my keeper."

"Then you too shall die once you are forgotten," said Lord Seb with sudden sadness as Oshun quickly continued.

"How can you demand the dead to honor a lord consumed with hate and revenge? Why would a lord pass judgment, only to then put them into an army? This cannot be your role," pleaded Lady Oshun.

"Your role is to grant and guide each to a healthy and joyful world if they are worthy of earning their cycle of growth," concluded Oshun.

"That role was taken from me when the late king removed my name and image from the halls of knowledge and banished me into this coffin," shouted Lord Seb.

"How could you not know?"

Lady Oshun took a step back from the cage wall and shook her head in disbelief. Now she understood why her people had become suspicious and fearful in their daily life. They would not receive guidance into their next life mission. Nor lessons by their lord of the underworld, and future consequences would remain uncertain."

Lady Oshun stepped forward and spoke again.

"I knew nothing of this," she said.

"The late king has always believed in our roles. Why would he have you removed?"

Lord Seb cleared his throat before speaking up again.

"The king decided he no longer believed in the passage and guidance of the dead. He exercised his power to abolish the process. Thankfully, I have been rescued by the high healer who has assisted in restoring my being. He will seek to convince the queen to reinstate me into the halls of knowledge with you as ransom. Finally, if she is not swayed by the depletion of crops from your lack of devotion, then I will wage war on her with my army."

Lady Oshun nodded and then responded with compassion.

"And because of a mortal decision you have chosen to enslave my people? Open your eyes to the power of love you have been gifted with and state your case to the queen. Revenge and war are beneath you. Only then will I honor you, Lord Seb. I wish to do what I can to convince the queen of the importance of your role to her people."

"I have heard enough! You do not know my pain, nor do you know the loneliness of being forgotten and replaced by an earthly queen. She is the one who now professes to have power over death and afterlife. It is not her gift. It does not belong to her, and she will pay!"

Lord Seb stood with his arms stretched over the lifeless forms in the pit.

"Sleep and your devotion will fill me once more."

Notti watched as the mortal dead slipped down to sit. Lord Seb placed his hands on a large stone, and instantly it pulled apart for him so he could walk through. He descended towards the dark pool and dove into the water. He quickly kicked up his heels and swam through the corridor. Guards stood at attention, while not moving an inch. Only with their eyes did they follow their lord until he was gone, they could now stand at ease until the morning when he would return once again with the newly deceased.

Chapter Twenty-Six

THE SPELL

A dead silence filled the air of the tomb with sorrow and mourning, as all slept while awaiting their judgement. Notti shuddered and sat down not knowing what to do.

"Who is there?" asked Lady Oshun, while peering through the cage.

"I can feel your presence. Come out now, for Lord Seb will not return until dawn."

Notti looked first at the dead and then at Lady Oshun's tomb.

"Come, and do not be afraid. I know you are here. I can feel your goodness. Do not worry about the guards; they are asleep, so speak to me."

Notti sighed and took a deep breath of courage.

"Yes, I am here. I'm on the balcony," said Notti with a little tremor in her voice.

"Walk to the end of the balcony and down the steps just behind me," answered Lady Oshun.

Notti crept along the curve of the balcony until she came to the steps. She trembled slightly at its narrow and steep decline with no railings.

"Good, now come down and we'll see if you can help me out of this prison," said Oshun.

Notti took careful steps and tried not to think about anything but getting down safely. Reaching the ground at last, she stepped quietly around each pit and dared not to look inside. Slowly, she tiptoed to the tomb and nearly jumped out of her sandals when two fingers poked through the cage and waved to her.

"I am here; can you see me?"

Notti looked through an opening and nodded.

"Yes, where am I?" Notti managed to ask.

"You are in one of the tombs of the dead where Lord Seb is preparing them for his kingdom," she said in her hushed and weakened voice.

"I am dying and desperately need help. What is your name and how did you come here?"

"My name is Notti, and I was sent here by Lady May Ya with my friends Prince Tuthra and Princes Zinga to find you."

"You must tell me everything you know, but first I need your help to get me out of here. Will you help me?"

"Yes, of course, I'll do my best, but I don't know what to do. How did you get in there?"

"Lord Seb imprisoned me when War Ma, the high seer and his goons invaded my temple," said Lady Oshun sorrowfully.

"How terrible, I'm so sorry, but what can I do?"

"Notti, there is a great deal you can do. Now listen to me and do as I say."

Notti put her ear up to the cage and listened to Lady Oshun's plan, just as the dawn began to rapidly approach.

*   *

*

Tuthra stirred and turned his neck to relieve a cramp. He awoke suddenly, and nearly knocked Zinga over, but caught her as she stirred. He rubbed his eyes in the dim light of the fading torch. There came a squeak from inside the pit. Zinga awoke, jolted by the sound, and reached for Tuthra's hand.

"Who is there?" demanded Tuthra, looking up at the gate,

"Show yourself," he continued, while shielding Zinga behind him. The squeaking continued, but the gate remained

179

closed. Zinga and Tuthra looked down to see water pouring into their pit.

"Have I slept too long?" asked Tuthra.

"Has our fate been decided?" cried Zinga.

"Look, the water is coming in from the tunnel," shouted Tuthra.

"There must be another gate!"

"And what of the crocodiles, can they be coming in too," said Zinga clutching his arm.

"We would do better out there than in here waiting for our death. Come, Zinga, we will try to escape through the tunnel."

Tuthra stood and reached for the torch. Zinga followed close behind, as they stepped swiftly through the rushing water. They guided themselves along the side walls and watched for any movement beneath them. Tuthra pulled Zinga back against the wall just as the shadow of a figure cast itself in front of them. Tuthra handed Zinga the torch and crouched down to wait as the shadow grew closer. Tuthra leaped and grabbed the figure, pulling it down into the water.

"What are you doing? Let me go," said a familiar voice.

"Notti!" cheered Zinga. "It is Notti."

Tuthra pulled her up, dripping and sputtering. They all wrapped their arms around each other and laughed.

"I'm so happy to see you," said Notti. "Are you alright?"

"Yes, we are," said Zinga, with her arms still wrapped around her.

"We were afraid that Lord Seb had you entombed."

Notti sighed in the arms of her friend and felt thankful that they weren't harmed.

"We have to hurry," said Notti pulling away.

"Follow me and press your gems for your tail and webbed feet. We have to swim a little way, so come on."

Zinga shook her head and asked, "what about the crocodiles?"

"Don't worry about them, they're on our side now," Notti said with a smile.

Tuthra and Zinga looked at each other curiously but followed anyway. They walked until the water reached their waists, they pressed on their gems and dove in. Their legs each became one, and once again they were granted tails.

"Where are we going," thought Zinga to Notti.

"We're going to a place not far from here, and near the entrance to Lord Seb's kingdom."

"Oh no," came Tuthra's worried thought.

"We are trying to get away from him. What reason could you have to take us there?"

"You'll see," thought Notti.

They reached the entrance of the tomb and were met by a circle of crocodiles swimming on the surface of the river. Notti went straight up to them with arms outstretched.

"Notti, come back." screamed Zinga's thought.

Tuthra swam after her, but Notti stopped just outside of the reptile circle and began humming a song. Tuthra caught up to her, but could only watch as the crocodiles circled, swimming faster and faster. Zinga and Tuthra were transfixed watching the reptiles swim so fast that their bodies appeared to join and became one large green ring.

Notti continued her song and concentrated on the reptiles, and never turning her eyes away. Zinga knew at once that something special had happened to Notti in Lord Seb's tomb.

From inside the green circle, there suddenly shot out a fish-tailed man, followed by a dozen tailed men and women. They rushed up to Notti with glowing swords strapped to their backs and holding silver shields.

"Thank you for your help. We are Lady Oshun's personal guards and are ready to help rescue our lady," thought one guard as he pointed his sword of light in front of him.

"You're welcome," thought Notti.

"My name is Notti, and these are my friends Prince Tuthra and Princess Zinga."

One guard nodded, before speaking.

"Follow us with caution to the entrance."

Notti nodded, but felt her stomach tighten as her thoughts went back to the battle of the painted men and the attack of the Kermas. She didn't want to see conflict or blood again. They all followed close behind the soldiers and around a large rock formation which brought them to the entrance of the tomb. Hiding behind the boulders, waited Lady Oshun's soldiers. Notti swam up to the surface and into the entrance. Waving her arms at a row of Lord Seb's guards, she shouted.

"Hello, hello, it's me again. I just came to say good-bye before I leave for home," she said nervously.

"Come here you wicked girl," shouted the first guard as he drew his sword and dove into the water. The others followed and they sped toward her just as the old woman had said they could. Suddenly panicked, Notti screamed and dove back in.

"They're coming, they're coming," she thought to the others as she dove deeper and swam faster. Lady Oshun's soldiers charged Lord Seb's guards, and Notti dodged to the right of the soldiers as she clearly heard the thoughts of two guards.

"It's Oshun's soldiers," thought one.

"The spell has been broken," thought the other, who immediately dropped his sword and fled through the river.

Chapter Twenty-Seven

THE RESCUE

Swords clashed and beams of light rippled throughout the turned-up waters. Red lights surged from Lady Oshun's soldiers, and white lights responded in defense from Lord Seb's guards. Tuthra rushed to grab the sword dropped by a fleeing guard, just as another guard dove towards him. Tuthra turned in time to plunge the sword into the guard's chest, and instantly white light filtered through the guard, and he beamed like a bulb before floating to the surface for a breath. Amazed that he wasn't killed, Tuthra swam to the surface and watched as the guard remained motionless but beaming.

Zinga followed Notti, and the two swam along the sides of the canal. Then up to the surface where a large rock statue of a crocodile stood. Notti rushed towards it and brushed her hands against the rock, while she sang a song of notes. Zinga watched in awe as the rock began to crack and crumble. A steam-like mist poured from the rubble and into a mushroomed cloud. From the cloud swam a dozen tailed men and women with swords of light. They too bowed and thanked Notti for breaking the spell.

The girls followed Lady Oshun's soldiers back into the tomb and immediately saw that the fighting had become fierce. More of Lord Seb's army appeared through the rock crevasses. They pushed Lady Oshun's soldiers back through the shallow canal and deeper into the river.

"We will lure them out into deeper water so you can get past. Six of us will follow you while the others continue the fight," thought one of Lady Oshun's soldiers.

Tuthra joined Notti and Zinga, and together they swam around the attack. They pulled themselves up like seals on to flat rocks near the entrance. When their legs and toes returned, they followed Notti to the rock wall, and she touched it.

"Ouch," she cried pulling her hand back.

"It's hot. Tuthra, will you put the sword tip into that crack?"

She pointed to a deep crack in the wall, and Tuthra stuck the tip inside. There was no more convincing needed to realize that Notti knew what she was doing.

"Together, we need to hold the sword and say, we demand that you open for us," said Notti. An air of confidence suddenly went through her. Zinga placed her hand on top of Tuthra's, and Notti held on to the very end of the sword.

"Okay, say it until it opens," shouted Notti.

"We demand that you open for us! We demand that you open for us." They repeated over and over again. Slowly and almost reluctantly, the crack began to grow wider and wider. A portion of the crack collapsed and crumbled. Bit by bit the hole became larger. Heat and stench billowed out, and everyone coughed and covered their faces as one by one they dashed in. Three of Lady Oshun's soldiers followed behind, just as Notti cried out.

"Everyone, fall on your bellies."

A beam of orange light poured out through the hole with such a force that the wall shook.

"What was that?" asked Tuthra.

"I don't know, but I saw it over there," said Notti as she pointed to blazing fire pits.

Notti stood and the others followed as she made her way past the pits. Zinga suddenly screamed and Tuthra gasped when they saw the shadowed dead in the large pits.

"What is this madness?" cried Tuthra.

"It is your people," said a soldier as they rushed towards Lady Oshun's tomb. The soldiers encircled the tomb, and in unison fell to one knee, bowing to their lady.

"We await your command," said the soldiers.

"Release me with your swords of light. Draw upon my love through Notti and her companions to break the spell surrounding me."

Notti, Zinga, and Tuthra stepped into the circle.

"It's Lady Oshun," said Zinga. "You found her Notti, you found her."

Notti smiled and pulled the leather band away from her bracelet and pointed to the green gem on her bracelet.

"You'll need this one to help Lady Oshun out of this tomb," whispered Notti.

Zinga and Tuthra nodded, as the soldiers concentrated on the children. Notti thought of Lady Oshun and of her beauty and love for the people of the valley. She envisioned the children, the slaves, Wara and her attendants, her new friends, and finally her grandfather.

Her gem glowed as the love flowed through her, building, and building until she thought she would burst. Zinga and Tuthra held Notti's hands and felt the outpouring of her love pass through them.

Raising their swords, the guards pointed them towards Lady Oshun's tomb while Notti held her vision. Notti softly sang her song filled with healing sounds, and immediately the swords lit up brighter than any had ever witnessed. The light rose and encircled the tomb into a golden ring. It penetrated the tomb and heated the stones, turning them into a brilliant orange. Instinctively, everyone took a step back just as the heat came over them like a wave. Slowly, the top portion of the tomb melted away and an opening was made.

"Stand back," cried Lady Oshun, with a voice that seemed to have come back to life.

The soldiers took another step back. Suddenly, there came a crash, and the tomb collapsed falling away into a large pile. From the rubble floated up the radiant lady, with not only beauty and grace, but with a brilliant blue light surrounding her. She looked into Notti's eyes.

"Thank you, Notti!"

"You're welcome," said Notti, still dazed, but grateful she had done everything Lady Oshun had asked her to do.

"But I couldn't have done it without the help of my friends. This is Tuthra and Zinga."

"I am honored to meet you both, and I am thankful for your help in my rescue."

"We are also honored," said Zinga and Tuthra.

"Now once again we must all work together, as Lord Seb will soon return. As we speak, he is making his way back," said Lady Oshun.

Her eyes looked weary, but a smile adorned her thin golden face. Floating over the pits, she raised her hands with palms up and spoke gently but with a powerful presence.

"Hear my call, sons, and daughters of this land. You have fallen victim to a lord who has lost his honor. Come with me now as we work to restore balance and peace to you before you enter the world of mortals or the world of the ancestors."

Lady Oshun's soldiers swung their swords of light over each pit until they were all aglow.
"Notti, open the passage to Lord Seb's tomb," requested Lady Oshun.

Notti ran to a far wall and counted each stone until she came to the tenth one. Placing both hands on the stone, she closed her eyes, sang her chant, and gently pushed. A large arched door emerged, and Notti stepped back as the door creaked open.

"To Lord Seb's underworld," ordered Lady Oshun to the dead.

No longer were the dead mere shadows, for now they rose from the pits with renewed energy. They hurried through the passage from Lord Seb's tomb into the underworld. Their exodus created a gust of wind and cooled and dispersed the tomb of any remaining odors.

"Follow them now to ensure their safe arrival, "said Lady Oshun. She pointed to two of her soldiers, who immediately dashed in after the dead.

"Two more of you will take up hidden positions on the balcony to await Lord Seb's arrival. He must not be allowed to leave the tomb," Lady Oshun concluded.

"What shall we do?" asked Tuthra.

"You shall come with me, along with the remaining two of my soldiers," she said with a sincere smile.

"Do you remember what to do?" asked Lady Oshun to Notti.

"Yes, I remember, because we're going another way to the underworld," replied Notti.

Behind the rubble of Lady Oshun's prison stood an ordinary stone wall. Notti placed her hands upon it, and another door appeared. Notti recited her chant, and the door opened.

"We will leave the door open for Lord Seb," Lady Oshun told her soldiers.
Notti grabbed a torch from the entrance and lit the way.
"Notti where does this lead to?" asked Tuthra.
"Lady Oshun told me that it's a passage around another tomb that's just over Lord Seb's underworld," she said compassionately.

"Which other tomb is that?" he pressed. Notti blinked rapidly and sighed before speaking.

"Your father's," she replied somberly.

Tuthra said nothing, as they continued. Steadily going up and turning many corners until the passage began to widen. The walls were raised higher to show a large double door. With beautiful paintings of scenes from the Oshun Valley. There were funeral processions, and mummies being placed in tombs with their many possessions. Tuthra walked up to the door and bowed his head. Zinga placed her hand on his shoulder and Notti slipped her hand into his.

"This is where he rests," said Tuthra in tears. Lady Oshun and her soldiers caught up to the three just as a thunderous roar exploded through the passageway.

"He's here, so go quickly to the tomb door," said Lady Oshun.

Tuthra wiped away his tears, and Zinga covered her mouth to keep from gasping. Notti could feel her heart pounding at the thought of the beastly lord on their heels. They ran while Lady Oshun floated with them in haste. They reached the end where a large wall stood painted with a dark figure.

The figure was of Lord Seb sitting on his throne and looking down on all those who would enter his world. Notti placed her hands on the door and again sang her chant. As she concentrated and repeated the words that Lady Oshun had taught her. The door opened, and once again dust billowed out as they raced in.

Chapter Twenty-Eight

INTO THE LIGHT

"Hurry," said Lady Oshun as she floated over and ahead of the party.

Her eyes sparkled as she flew with delight and reverence, to all who had helped to rescue her from the now bellowing lord of the underworld.

"Where are you taking us to," chimed in Zinga and Tuthra together?

"Down into Lord Seb's original tomb," replied Lady Oshun.

The tunnel widened, allowing the party to pass through with ease and speed.

"What do you mean by original tomb?" asked Zinga.

"The original tomb where he reigned before his banishment from the Wall of Knowledge," she said with a hint of sadness.

Notti and Zinga looked at each other, and Zinga suddenly knew that it would be best to keep quiet and trust Lady Oshun's plan. So much had taken place in such a short amount of time, and evidently there was still much more to come.

The tunnel narrowed again, and they were forced to continue in a single file, with Lady Oshun lighting the way and her soldiers following behind. Notti found herself almost out of breath trying to keep up. She took a couple of deep breaths and watched her steps closely as the tunnel began to descend.

"We're almost there everyone, the second entrance is just after this turn," said Lady Oshun. Just then another booming voice echoed through them.
"Oshun, you have no right, no right I say to you."
"He's closer," said Tuthra with a worried expression that bordered between fear and dread.

"What will he do if he catches us?" asked Zinga, equally frightened.

"No time to think of such things," said Lady Oshun. She swooped down and stepped on to the path in front of Notti.

"We're here," she said, standing before a large double door.

Instantly, Lady Oshun's bluish glow faded. She materialized from light into form.

Notti observed the tomb walls with paintings of the river people. There were scenes of the dead passing through many doors, before reaching a final door of light. Another scene showed Lord Seb pointing up with his right hand toward the people consumed in light. Also, down with his left hand toward the people farming in the valley. Lady Oshun approached the door, and with her hands she firmly pushed the door open.

"An entrance to my river is just beyond these doors," she whispered.

She stepped inside and floated toward the center of the tomb, while the others followed. From an opening in the far corner, her soldiers led the dead onto a large platform to wait.

"Take your positions," said Lady Oshun, as she stepped on the platform and sat upon a throne before the dead souls.

"Where should we go?" asked Zinga.

"You'll leave through there," said Lady Oshun, pointing to the far-right wall with more images and scenes of the dead.

"There you'll find another tunnel leading back into King Mene's tomb, and from there you will make your way out."

"It is forbidden for anyone to enter the tomb of my father," said Tuthra.

"We have no choice," said Notti. "It's our only way out."
With despair clouding his eyes, Tuthra turned to Lady Oshun as she spoke.
"Please let go of your fear Tuthra. Your father has already passed judgment and is residing with the ancestors. You will not

disturb him by passing through his tomb. And to bring further comfort to you, I will tell you of his destiny. It has been declared that a child will be born among our people who will fulfill the role of Master Shu's apprentice. Thus continuing the practice and teachings of the ancient knowledge of the dreamtime. That child will carry your father's energy. Do you understand?"
Tuthra nodded that he understood and sighed with relief.

"So, people can come back?" asked Notti with an air of both awe and disbelief.

"Yes, if it is by ancestral guides who oversee the soul's development," said Lady Oshun.

"O – S – H – U- N," bellowed Lord Seb's call of rage through the tunnel.

"He is almost here, now go. Farewell Notti and thank you for my rescue. I will always be watching you."

"Good-bye Lady Oshun, I will never forget you and what you taught me. Thank you," said Notti as quickly as she could.

They kissed and embraced, and Notti stepped aside to let Zinga and Tuthra say their goodbyes. Zinga bowed and kissed Lady Oshun's cheek, as did Tuthra.

"Prince Tuthra, my gift to you is this. When you return, tell our people you have spoken to me. As proof of our alliance, you will ask the river to flood the fields with fertile silt two seasons out of four. This will be a small punishment for their disrespect of their neighbors, and for their lack of gratitude for the natural gifts given to them from me and from the valley.

"O-S-H-U-N," called Lord Seb again.

Lady Oshun continued to speak above Lord Seb's roar.

"If in-between the seasons, the people show a willingness to accept and change their ways, you may call upon me. I will overflow with abundance each season. When the people see this, they will respect you and your mother's power to govern this land in peace."

A pounding echo bounced along the tunnel walls.

"He is here. Quickly, through the doors, go now. Do not worry, he will agree to my terms. We will drive out his madness with the help of the ancestors, and a healing light," she concluded. She gave her soldiers a nod as they drew their glowing swords.

Notti and her friends raced off the platform to the painted wall. Notti placed her hands on the tenth stone and the metal doors opened and they rushed through into another dark tomb.

Tuthra drew his sword of light, and they all turned back to see Lord Seb's shadowy figure enter the tomb, just as the door closed tightly and disappeared back into the wall.

"Let's go," said Notti with a renewed enthusiasm in her heart.

"We should have stayed and helped Lady Oshun," said Tuthra.

"I agree," said Zinga. "What if his anger is too powerful?"

"Don't worry; Lady Oshun will know how to help him. Now that she's free she can use her own powers, so come on let's get out of here," insisted Notti.

Tuthra offered Notti his lit sword; Notti smiled and grabbed it. She took a couple of skips then held the sword up high like the leader of a marching band, as Zinga and Tuthra followed.

"I can't believe what we just did. I mean, who would believe we just helped the real lady of the river? Now that I think about it, nobody would believe it, so I guess it will always be our secret, right?" said Notti as she shrugged her shoulders.

When no one answered, Notti turned around to see Tuthra and Zinga standing by a platform.

"What's the matter with you two?" she said, running back. Why aren't you happy? We did what Lady Oshun asked us to do."

"It's not that, Notti," said Zinga.

"It's my father," replied Tuthra.

Notti raised the sword, allowing the light to be cast on a grave, as Zinga and Tuthra knelt.

"Please forgive us Father for disturbing your resting place," said Tuthra.

Slowly they rose and took a step back, and Notti could see tears on Tuthra's cheeks.

"I realize after all we've been through; how much I miss him. If only he were alive today. This gift from Lady Oshun would be his. He should still be governing our people."

"That's not true," said Zinga. "Your father left you to some ay be king because he believed in you, and so does Lady Oshun."

"I agree with Zinga," said Notti. "You can be king to her people, and hopefully you can persuade your mother the queen as well. Just remember what she told you. Now come on, I want to get out of these clothes, eat some more of that great food we had before, and get home."

Tuthra and Zinga smiled.

"You are quite remarkable," said Tuthra. "I am grateful for the encouragement. Lead the way, we are behind you."

Though the tomb appeared to be smaller than Lord Seb's, it still contained elaborate and decorative symbols and writings on the walls. They had a short walk before they came to another wall.

Notti handed Tuthra the sword and placed her hands on the two symbols of a man and a woman. She recited her words and stood back. Nothing happened, so she tried it again. Still nothing happened.

"Oh no, I think I forgot which symbol opens this door, but how could I? It's so simple. Oh, what do I do now? Nobody knows we're in here."

"Dear Notti, please calm down," said Zinga as she rushed to her side.

"Why did you pick these two symbols?"

"Because Lady Oshun said it would be two figures, one female and the other a male. And that's what these are."

Zinga looked closely at the wall and followed her hand over all the symbols, until she came across another that looked smaller, but almost identical to the ones Notti chose.

"Try this one," said Zinga.

Notti had to stand on her tiptoes to place her hands on the symbols and recite the words. A door instantly appeared and opened. Notti sighed and they all laughed and hugged each other.

"Zinga, how did you know which ones they were?"

"Well, when Lady Oshun said male and female, she must have been speaking of children, not adults. These are the symbols for children."

One by one they stepped through the unusually small door and followed the path to the entrance. Notti felt her feet dragging and a sudden wave of fatigue came over her. The three finally emerged into the dawn. The light reflected off their tired faces, and they realized they had spent the entire night in the tombs.

"I'm really tired," said Notti looking at the long road leading back to the village.
"Yes, I am as well. What a shame that we have to walk all the way back" replied Tuthra.

Notti's eyes suddenly lit up. "We may not have to walk after all, because I just remembered something my friend Patrick said."

Running down the stone steps, she cupped her hands around her mouth and took a deep breath. "Lightning, come to me," she called.

Zinga and Tuthra looked at each other curiously but followed her and stood by her side. Within the time it takes to jump up and down six times with glee, the sound of galloping and neighs could be heard.

"Lightning, over here. We're over here!" Notti shouted as she waved the sword in circles and did a jig her grandpa had taught her.

"You came back for me, you wonderful horse," she said grabbing his reins and steadying him. Suddenly there came the sound of more galloping, and a moment of panic filled Tuthra as he thought of his mother. But before they could react, up trotted Tuthra and Zinga's horses, and once again there was relief, laughter, and more hugs.

Tuthra helped Notti and Zinga up onto their saddles, before jumping onto his own. Notti leaned over and whispered into Lightning's ear.

"Mighty horse, take us to the temple of Prince Tuthra, now!"

Lightning lifted his front legs while Notti held on tight. Off they streaked toward the village that would soon awaken to delicate rays of sunlight. Light that would touch everything on its path with gentle kisses of dew.

Notti leaned over and hugged Lightning with a sigh. It all seemed so unbelievable and too magical to have been real. There was no denying it, they had done well. Now there was hope for a change and a new beginning. Notti's eyelids grew heavier as once again she felt her fatigue. They rode with speed and with ease, and she looked down several times to see if she was floating above the ground. However, it was just Lightning's power carrying her along with his grace.

Notti shivered as she thought of what might be waiting for them at the temple. She suddenly feared for Tuthra's life and glanced at him sitting proudly in his saddle. Thoughts of retaliation came to her. What if his mother throws him into prison? What if she throws them all into prison? The fears began to build, but instead of panicking, she whispered into Lightning's ear.

"When we reach the temple, go right to the stairs as fast as you can, so no one can stop us." Notti closed her eyes and thought of Lady Oshun. Holding a clear image in her mind of the floating lady, Notti made her plea.

"Dear Lady Oshun, please protect Tuthra. I am afraid his mother will hurt him."

She opened her eyes to see the third gem shining on her bracelet, and sighed with relief, knowing Lady Oshun heard her message.

Lightning lived up to his name, for they were already on the outskirts of the village. He neither stopped nor slowed down as they entered and passed many villagers making their way to the market. Notti rode up the hill toward the temple and raced past the guards. They had no time to react to the bolt of light that galloped through the grounds. Neither Lightning nor the two other horses stopped until they reached the palace steps. Once they did stop, they were quickly surrounded by the palace guards.

"It is the prince and princes" cried one of the guards.
"He's alive," cried another. Tuthra's baldheaded aide came running out of the door and down the stairs.
"Your mother said you drowned in the river," he said. "We are thankful for your return to us, dear Tuthra."

"Where is my mother?" asked Tuthra, ignoring his praise.

"She will announce to all at the arena, that she will continue to be the reigning queen."

Tuthra grimaced and shook his head. Notti and Zinga looked at each other and nodded, knowing their suspicions were correct.

"And where is Master Shu?" continued Tuthra.

"He is with her. She wants the people to see that even the old master supports her appointment," concluded the aide.

Tuthra turned to Notti and Zinga.

"I will return as soon as I can," he said softly. "I must stop my mother and deliver Lady Oshun's message. Notti, may I please borrow Lightning?"

"Of course, and good luck," she said sincerely.

"We'll celebrate when you return," said Zinga with a reassuring smile.

"Please escort the young ladies to their chambers," said Tuthra to the maidans.

Notti and Zinga were helped down by the guards, and when the two slid off and looked at each other, they laughed at the sight of their hair and clothes.

"We're a mess," giggled Notti.

She held Lightning's head in her hands and whispered in his ear.

"Take Prince Tuthra now and obey his commands and no one else until you come back to me."

Tuthra mounted Lightning, and left, followed by half a dozen soldiers. Notti and Zinga waved and watched him until he disappeared down the hill. They followed the maidans up the extensive flight of stairs, down the long and beautiful hallway, and finally to the doors of their elegant room. One maidan opened the door for them, and without thinking, Notti and Zinga tried to enter the room at the same time. Zinga laughed and shook her head.

"Look at us. We must be very tired. After you," Zinga said affectionately.

"Why, thank you," replied Notti. "I know I'm tired, but the first thing I'm going to do is to get into that big tub of warm water and soak. My legs better not turn into a dolphin tail either."

They both laughed so hard that they had to hold their sides. The maidan bowed with curiosity before leaving them. The girls undressed everything except for their bags of gems.

Soon the girls were slipping into their oil-scented tubs, relaxing, and putting their fears and concerns behind them. Zinga suddenly perked up and leaned over towards Notti.

"I expect you will want to return home, now that we've completed our mission?"

"Well, as much as I would love to stay, I really do think I need to get home," replied Notti.

"I will miss you, Notti," she continued as she closed her eyes.

I'm going to miss you too and will just soak for a few more minutes."

The moments turned into several more until she felt herself falling asleep and into a dream of

Grandpa Pine

Chapter Twenty-Nine

SUNFISH AND BLUEGILLS

Notti awoke suddenly and found herself swimming through a school of sunfish. They darted suddenly toward a glimmering object. With intrigue, Notti couldn't help but follow. She caught up to them with little effort. When she looked down, she was stunned to realize that she was naked. Oh, my goodness she thought, wrapping her arms over her budding chest.

"What am I going to do?"

The sunfish scattered in all directions, except for one who thrashed about from side to side as it slowly rose toward the surface beneath a drifting shadow.

"It's a boat," she thought as she quickly swam to the surface and stuck her head out just in time to see the fish fly into the air.

"Ha, ha," came a familiar voice, followed by a joyful laugh. A boat slowly drifted around, and a hand pulled the fish up and attached it to the rest of the catch. Finally, the fisherman turned around and looked down upon Notti with gentle and beaming eyes. With surprise, Notti's mouth dropped open and filled up with water, which sent her into a coughing fit.

"Notti, Notti, is that you?

She nodded as water sputtered out of her nose and mouth.

"Thank goodness you made it through. Come on, swim over here and let me pull you in."

Notti finally caught her breath and swam until she reached the boat and waited. Grandpa sensed her discomfort and grabbed a towel, which he held up while she climbed in. Once inside the boat, Notti wrapped herself in the towel and then embraced by Grandfather's loving arms.

"Well done, Notti. I knew you could do it."

"Thank you, Grandpa, I'm so glad to see you. I've missed you and so has Grandma."

"I've missed you both too Sweetheart."

Notti pulled herself away and gazed at his sparkling tear-filled eyes. She looked around at her surroundings and sighed.

"I'm back home?" she stuttered, and her eyes also filled with tears of joy and appreciation.

They were on the small lake by the Witch's Tower, so she knew she was home, yet felt confused.

"If you're here with me, then am I also still in the dreamtime?"

"I'm here so I could call you back. In the dreamtime, someone must call you back. That's why it's important to keep the memory of the ancestors alive. If you don't remember us, then we can't help you. You must keep us in your heart because it's your love that helps me to communicate with you. What you just did is wonderful, Notti.

By helping to restore Lord Seb's name again on to the temple walls, the people were able to carry on his memory in the light he was meant to fulfill. They will treat him now as Father Earth of the underworld. He will be a nurturing and caring lord. You and your friends helped to restore a very sacred process."

"Wow, that's amazing, Grandpa," said Notti, as he pulled in his stringer of fish into the boat.

"While I was waiting for you, I decided to do a little fishing," he chuckled.

"Take these sunfish and bluegills with you and ask your mom to fry them up for breakfast.

I know you're hungry after your long journey."

With the oars, he steered the boat to shore, until the bottom rubbed up against the weeds.

"Well, this is your stop, so all a shore who is going ashore."

Notti climbed out and Grandpa handed her the stringer of fish. He gave her a salute before pushing off.

"Grandpa, wait! Don't leave, I don't have any clothes," she said looking around and hoping they would have washed up on the shore somewhere. The sun had only just come up, so the neighborhood was still quiet and empty. At any moment someone could show up and walk by, she thought. How was she going to explain herself, standing there wrapped in a towel, and holding a stringer of fish?

"You'll be okay, don't worry, you'll think of something, and I'll be watching," said Grandpa.

In a flash of light, he and his rowboat faded away. Notti stood blinking back her tears. She whispered thanks for seeing her grandpa and wondered when she would see him again. Then she remembered something she had wanted to say to him.

"Thank you for the bracelet," she shouted to the empty lake.

"Notti," a familiar voice called.

Notti strained to see, but the person was hidden behind several oak trees.

"Who is it?" she called back.

"It's me Patrick, who else would be looking for you?"

He casually stepped out and away from the trees with a welcoming smile.

Notti relaxed a bit, realizing Patrick would at least try to understand her humiliating dilemma. She watched him shaking his head as he looked at his silly friend. Notti felt embarrassed, but while still holding on to her towel, she thought of changing her story a bit to avoid being teased.

"I'll just tell him I took my clothes off to take a swim, and when I got out, they were gone," she thought.

Notti laughed at herself as she thought of what really happened, and how only moments ago she was taking a bath and saying goodbye to her friend Zinga. As she envisioned Zinga and remembered her pouch of gems. She pulled back her wristband to find it tightly on her wrist. With another sigh of relief, she smiled and was thankful for her amazing gift.

She thought Lady Oshun and would have liked to see her again. To tell her that despite having been captured by the Kerma's, she was glad to have helped. Notti knew she would not hesitate if she were summoned again. The experience was initially very frightening. Her life had changed and become something beyond her dreams.

Patrick stepped quietly in front of Notti, knowing she was deep in thought. He held in his chuckle and waited until their eyes met.

"What day is it and how long have I been gone?"

"Well, it's it is very early Sunday morning, and Hanna and I both saw you this Saturday at the Witches tower. Right after those people came out of the bright light, you disappeared. We looked for you everywhere, and then we went to Aunt Lizzy's house."

"How did you know I was here," she asked, realizing his appearance was a coincidence.

"I had a dream that you would be at the lake and would need help. I stopped by Hanna's house on the way here and told her you'd need some clothes," he said handing her a plastic bag.
"Thank you, Patrick, for helping me, and for being my friend."
"You're welcome; anytime!"

Notti handed Patrick the stringer of fish and took the bag. She ran behind a large tree, half surrounded by lilac bushes. Inside the bag she found a pair of shorts and a T-shirt. Quickly, she scrambled into them and carefully folded up her towel. Patrick nodded his approval when she stepped out from behind the tree.

"I want to hear all about what happened, and so does Hanna and Aunt Lizzy. Hanna wants to know if you can meet her at Aunt Lizzy's house for lunch?"

"Yes, I will come for lunch and tell her everything that happened and what I learned."

The sunfish and bluegills started flapping, and the bracelet gem glowed.

"I think that's a good sign," she said with a smile.

I better get home before my parents get up. They always sleep in later Sunday mornings.

"I think so too," said Patrick with an even bigger smile.

"Is it okay if I tell them, you caught these fish for me this morning?"

"Yes Notti. I'll see you in school tomorrow. Bye"

"Bye Patrick and thank you and Hanna too."

THE END

Thank you for reading my story of Notti's adventures to becoming a light carrier,

Sincerely

Cherie Andrea Hamilton